''You **mother, Alison.''**

Clint spoke quietly, but she was caught by something in his voice.

She tensed. ''I'll never be a mother,'' she said. ''You know how I feel about men. I'll never get married.''

''You might change your mind.'' It was said so oddly, that her heart pounded suddenly in her chest.

''I'll never change it,'' she said, very firmly indeed.

Clint was still holding her hand, and now his other hand went to her face, his long fingers tracing a slow path around her lips.

He laughed softly, inflaming emotions that were already raw. ''I told you before that 'never' is a word I don't have in my vocabulary.''

Rosemary Carter began writing short stories that, for a long time, brought only rejections. The turnabout came at the end of her first pregnancy. "It's a memory I cherish," she says, "for the baby was born the day after the acceptance." She lives a few hours away from the Canadian Rockies, and she and her husband love exploring the beautiful mountain trails. But enchantment with her previous home has never waned, and that is why she sets most of her books in the South African bushveld.

Books by Rosemary Carter

HARLEQUIN ROMANCE

1986—MAN OF THE WILD
2312—RETURN TO DEVIL'S VIEW
2380—MAN IN THE SHADOWS
2816—WALK INTO TOMORROW

HARLEQUIN PRESENTS

615—LION'S DOMAIN
664—SERPENT IN PARADISE
752—LETTER FROM BRONZE MOUNTAIN
831—IMPETUOUS MARRIAGE
855—A FOREVER AFFAIR
880—PILLOW PORTRAITS

No Greater Joy

Rosemary Carter

Harlequin Books

TORONTO • NEW YORK • LONDON
AMSTERDAM • PARIS • SYDNEY • HAMBURG
STOCKHOLM • ATHENS • TOKYO • MILAN

Original hardcover edition published in 1988
by Mills & Boon Limited

ISBN 0-373-02965-9

Harlequin Romance first edition March 1989

CHAPTER ONE

ALISON had no idea how long the man had been watching her.

She was grooming her horse when something made her straighten and turn her head. Some sense that she was not alone in the stable-yard, and that someone was looking at her.

It was one of those glorious mornings when the sun stood high in the sky, and the long grasses of the African bushveld rippled in the wind. Girl and horse had had such a wonderful time galloping over *kopjes* and beside *vleis* that Alison had even been able to forget that anything existed beyond the harmony with the horse that had been her joy since her fifteenth birthday.

It was the sense that she was not alone which had pulled her back to reality.

The man was leaning against the white-railed fence of the paddock, a jacket slung across his shoulder, one leg crossed casually over the other. A stranger. The sun was behind him, so that Alison could not see his face but she didn't have to see his face to know that he would be attractive. There was a kind of animal sinuousness in that long, lean body which in itself was attractive.

A lithe movement brought him upright, and then he was coming towards her—a superbly built man, his gait long and loose and somehow uncompromising. Instinctively, Alison took a step backwards, momentarily stunned by a maleness which she sensed rather than

5

understood. And then she remembered who she was, and that this was her territory, and she stood her ground.

He had to be a customer, interested in boarding a horse, or something equally innocuous. But she was in no mood these days to talk to men, attractive ones in particular. She cast a quick look around the stables; let Dad do the talking. But her father was nowhere to be seen.

The man *was* attractive, she saw as he came closer—six feet two at least, with broad shoulders, narrow hips and long legs encased in faultlessly tailored trousers. He had the ruggedly tanned appearance of an outdoors person. His hair was thick and dark, his face all chiselled lines, and beneath winging brows his eyes were appraising. Tough, she decided, and very confident, as if he took life pretty much in his stride.

'Nice place you have here.' His voice was low and vital.

It so happened that Alison was in no mood for pleasantries, so she just said coolly, 'Can I help you?'

Something flickered briefly in his eyes, but his voice did not change. 'That depends. I'm looking for Miss Alison Lenox.'

'I am Alison Lenox.'

'I thought you might be.' He put out his right hand. 'Clint Demaine.'

Clint Demaine—the name was familiar.

Alison made herself take his hand. His grip was cool and firm, nothing in it to account for the quiver that shot unexpectedly up her arm. The sensation caused something to harden inside her, because with any sort of feeling came vulnerability, and she had made herself a promise that she would never be vulnerable again.

She frowned up at him. 'Mr Demaine...?'

'It's obvious you've forgotten.' He smiled down at her, an attractive, devil-may-care smile that warmed his eyes and deepened the laughter-lines which ran from nose to mouth. 'I wrote to you a few months ago, offering you a job.'

She remembered then. 'Of course—the children's adventure camp! You wanted me to take care of the horses and to lead the children on trail-rides through the mountains.'

'Right.'

'But I declined the offer, Mr Demaine.'

'To my regret. I don't mean to be personal, Miss Lenox, but...I gathered your refusal concerned a man?'

She hesitated only a moment. 'Yes.'

'Someone special in your life?'

She certainly owed him no explanation, this too attractive man who was unlikely to have any more compunction than Raymond about hurting a woman.

So she only said, 'In a way. Although I don't see what concern that is of yours, Mr Demaine.'

'It isn't.' A thoughtful look. 'Except that I was hoping you might reconsider my offer.'

'I don't think so—I'm sorry.'

'Because of your boyfriend?'

'Yes.' The lie was convenient.

There was an expression she could not read in the eyes that held hers. 'I'm sorry, too.'

When he made no move to go, she said, 'I don't understand, Mr Demaine. Surely you must have found someone else for the job by now?'

'There was someone, yes, but she hurt herself when her horse came to grief on a hurdle.'

Alison looked at him disbelievingly. 'And you came all this way on the offchance that I might change my mind?'

'I could have written or phoned,' he conceded, with that attractive smile. 'But since I had some business in the area, and have to spend a night in the village anyway, it seemed like a good idea to come and see you.'

'Well, I'm glad you didn't go out of your way,' she said politely. 'And I hope you still manage to find the right person.'

'I hope so too, Miss Lenox.'

There was an odd look in his eyes as he walked away.

'Something on your mind?' asked a voice at her side.

Alison turned to her sister, who had come up beside her at the paddock gate. 'I think I may just be the world's biggest idiot, Lynn.'

'Anything to do with the man who just drove off in that very expensive car?'

'That was Clint Demaine, the fellow who owns Bushveld Camp—the children's adventure camp.'

'Right! I remember the name. He offered you a job, didn't he?'

'Out of the blue, yes. Seems he'd heard that I'd worked at Morley's Camp two years running, doing pretty much the same things he'd have wanted me to do at his own camp, I suppose—working with children and horses. And when Morley's decided not to run the camp again this year, Jeff Morley gave Mr Demaine my name.'

'But you turned the offer down because...' Lynn's words died away.

'Because I thought Raymond and I were going to be married,' Alison said drily. 'It's OK, Lynn, don't feel so bad about it, you can't keep watching every word you say to me. And the same goes for Mom and Dad. All the family sympathy is well-meant...'

'But it's driving you up the wall?'

'It's beginning to get to me,' Alison admitted, blinking back a sudden rush of tears. She had done with crying! She didn't intend to shed another tear over Raymond Whitney, nor over any other man.

Lynn pretended not to notice her distress. 'What about this Clint Demaine? And what makes you the world's biggest idiot?'

'He came here to see if I might have had second thoughts about taking the job.'

'Oh?'

'I said no. I wasn't thinking too clearly.' Alison's expression was thoughtful.

'You mean you're sorry now?'

'When it's probably too late...yes.'

'You'd like to get away?' suggested Lynn.

'I'm impatient to start making a new life for myself. I can't wait to get out and begin my career.' Alison frowned. 'There's Raymond's wedding too, of course— I'd be less than honest if I said I'd be sorry to miss it, as well as all the fanfare leading up to it. Edna's dad is so well off, and she's an only child, they're going to make this an event people around here will talk about for ages.'

'I suppose so...' Lynn looked troubled.

'You must all go, of course,' insisted Alison. 'You and Mom and Dad.'

'You know we'll hate every moment.'

'Oh, I know that, but you can't stay away. The Lenoxes and the Whitneys have known each other since before you and I were born.'

'But *you* wouldn't have to subject yourself to it, Allie. Nobody could expect you to, nobody would be so cruel.'

'But my absence would be noted—and talked about. And so yes, if I'm here, I fully intend to go to Raymond's wedding, if only to show that I'm still alive and kicking.'

Alison was silent a moment. When she went on, she looked grim. 'I love this place—the village, the stables, the country life. But I get so impatient with the small-mindedness that goes along with it. Everyone knowing everyone else's business—the gossip, the stares every time I walk down the main street.'

'People will forget in time,' said Lynn comfortingly.

'Yes, I know. It's been a month since Raymond and I stopped seeing each other, so perhaps they're starting to forget already. Anyway, I can live with the gossip—even if I don't like it particularly.'

Lynn smiled. 'You always were the spunky one of us two.'

Alison grinned back at her. 'You're not too bad yourself, Sis!' And then her face grew serious. 'I'm restless, Lynn. I can't wait to get on with my life.'

'You still want stables of your own, then?'

'More than ever.'

'And that's why you're sorry you didn't take Clint Demaine up on his offer?'

'It would have been a first step, don't you see?' Alison explained. 'I've been thinking, Lynn, making plans. I still have all the money Gran left me, and I know Mom and Dad won't mind giving me a loan. I'll do the things we do here—board horses for other people, give lessons.

I know how to run a stable, and I think I could make a success of it.'

'I know you could.'

'Trouble is, I'm not yet quite ready for it. That's why I should have taken the job at Bushveld Camp. The salary is fantastic—I remember that from Clint Demaine's letter—and I'd be working with children and horses, the two things I adore.'

'You've convinced me.' Lynn, who hadn't seen her sister so excited about anything in too long a time, despite her brave words, was smiling. 'The thing I don't understand is why you refused Mr Demaine.'

'Put it down to my stupid habit of not reflecting before I react. I didn't give myself time to think.'

'I still don't understand.'

Alison looked at her sister, then away. 'He was just too much of everything. Too good-looking, too confident, probably too rich.'

'How do you know he's too rich?'

'You saw that glitzy piece of metal he calls a car.'

'I have a feeling you left out too sexy,' put in her sister, a little mischievously.

'That, too,' Alison said crossly.

'Did he make a pass at you?'

'Heavens, no, he was politeness itself. On the surface. But there was something in his eyes . . .' Alison stopped. 'Why are you smiling?'

'I'm glad that Raymond didn't spoil you for other men.'

'That's just it! The reason I said no to Mr Demaine. Raymond *did* spoil me.'

'Allie . . .' Lynn put out a tentative hand. 'It would be good for you to meet other men. You're not going to want to be alone for ever just because Raymond Whitney behaved like a swine.'

'Forget it!' Alison shot back fiercely. 'Raymond opened my eyes. I mean, Raymond, of all people! Sweet, gentle Raymond. Now that I know what men are capable of doing, I'll give no man the chance to hurt me again.'

Lynn was silent a moment before asking, 'Are you really telling me that all these thoughts went through your mind when you refused Clint Demaine's offer?'

Alison grinned at her. 'In condensed form. Stupid, wasn't it? It's not even as if I'd have anything to do with the man.'

Lynn was relieved to see a lightening of her sister's mood. 'Besides which, Mr Demaine might be married. Perhaps his wife will be at the camp, too.'

'Could be,' Alison shrugged. But Clint Demaine had not had the look of a married man.

'Are you going to take the job, Allie?'

'I'd like very much to give it a try. If I haven't ruined my chances, that is. Mr Demaine said something about spending the night in the village.'

'He'd have to be at the Flame Tree, then. The only other place is a dump. Will you phone him, Allie?'

'Might be better if I went to see him. Keep your fingers crossed for me, Lynn.'

It was impossible to miss seeing the sleek, silver-grey Porsche parked in the shade of the flame trees. But Clint Demaine did not answer his phone when the desk clerk rang through to his room. Alison glanced around the lounge, where several people were chatting over drinks, then she went outside and walked in the direction of the swimming-pool.

There was only one person in the water, and Alison knew at once that it was Clint. Shading her eyes against the glare, she watched him a few minutes. Clint Demaine was a strong swimmer and a joy to watch—style fluid and beautiful, arms and legs pushing a strong yet effortless path through the water, neat somersault turn when he came to the end of a length and began another.

He had done several lengths when he raised his head and saw her. White teeth glinted in a flash of recognition.

Something quivered inside Alison as he swam to the side and grinned wickedly up at her from the water. It was the oddest sensation.

'Hello, Alison.'

The use of her first name was unexpected, jolting her.

'Hello, Mr Demaine.' She licked lips that were dry all at once. 'I thought I'd come and talk to you. You see, I've decided...'

'Hold it!' he interrupted.

A lithe movement brought him out of the pool, then he was standing beside her. Involuntarily, Alison's gaze went to his body. Six feet two inches of overwhelming maleness; copper skin glistening; muscles in his arms and chest smooth beneath his tan; wet hair clinging to his head like a cap.

It was a moment or two before she managed to look away. She said, 'Mr Demaine...' and for some reason her voice was not quite steady.

'Nice,' he murmured, his eyes going over her in a look that was intensely male. 'Quite a transformation!'

Alison's cheeks were warm as her hand touched the dress she'd changed into before coming here—a simple dress, yet one which showed off her slender figure to perfection. 'I don't *live* in jeans, Mr Demaine.'

He laughed softly. 'With a figure like yours, I'm glad to hear it!'

She made her voice brisk. 'Look, Mr Demaine, I came here to talk to you.'

His eyes were sparkling. 'And talk we shall. Let's just find a place to sit first.'

Without waiting for an answer, he walked towards a couple of deck-chairs. After a moment, Alison followed him.

The chairs were close together, as if the people who had vacated them had been having an intimate conversation. A little too close for Alison's liking. She was about to move a chair when something made her glance at Clint Demaine.

His lips were tilted at the corners and his eyes were teasing. Darn the man! Lifting her chin, Alison allowed the chair to remain where it was, and sat down.

He sat down himself then in the chair beside hers, so close to her that his thighs were just a hand's reach from her own, and his bare, wet toes might have touched hers in their open sandals if she had not deliberately moved her feet beneath her chair.

'What can I get you, Alison? Coffee?' And when she shook her head, 'A beer? Something cold?'

'Nothing, thank you.'

'You said you wanted to talk,' he hinted.

'Yes...' Nervousness had made her throat dry, so that in a way she regretted her refusal of something to drink. 'I've changed my mind, Mr Demaine.'

'Oh?'

'I think I would like the job.'

'I see.'

She stared at him, beginning to feel more than a little unnerved. 'I wonder if the offer is still open.'

'What made you change your mind?' he asked.

'Is that really important?' Her voice was low.

'Put it down to interest,' he said mildly. 'A couple of hours ago you seemed adamant that the job wasn't for you, so now I'm interested. What made you change your mind?'

Unable to meet his probing gaze all at once, she looked down. His body was beginning to dry in the hot sun, and her eyes were riveted to his thighs. They were so taut, and for one appalling moment she wondered how the tanned skin would feel beneath her fingers.

'Well, Alison?'

She forced her eyes back to his. She had an uncomfortable feeling that her face was flushed.

'I realised...that I'd made a mistake,' she began.

'A mistake?'

Damn him! Did he have to make it quite so difficult for her?

'Well, yes. I thought I might not be able to get away from home at this time,' she improvised, 'but I was wrong. It's the kind of job I've always enjoyed. I loved working at Morley's Camp. And...'

'And?' he prompted.

'There's the money, of course.'

'Now, that's something I can understand,' he agreed.

'I love working with horses and children, Mr Demaine. Dad pays me what he can for the work I do at the stables, but I could do with some extra money.'

'Because you're going to be married?' There was an odd note in his tone.

Alison was on her feet in a second. 'What I do with my money is my own business!'

A cool hand reached for her wrist. She tried to jerk away, but Clint Demaine's grip was too strong for her.

'Let me go!' she ordered tersely.

'Sit down.'

'No!'

He stood up too now, the movement pulling her against him. His body was cool from the water, and his skin was still slightly damp. A distinctive male smell filled Alison's nostrils, so that for a moment she felt dizzy.

'Sit down,' he said again. 'Please.'

'There's no point.' Her throat hurt.

'I think there is.' His voice was so gentle now that after another moment she let herself be persuaded, and then he sat down, too.

He leaned towards her, his hand cupping her chin. 'I seem to have caught you on the raw with that last question. You were quite right, Alison, it's really none of my business what you do with your money. I'm sorry.'

Sorry was a word Raymond had never found it easy to say. Even after he'd hurt her.

'You haven't even said whether the offer's still open,' she muttered.

'Haven't I?' He laughed softly, so close to her that his breath fanned her hot cheek. 'Yes, Alison, the job is yours if you want it.'

'I do. Thank you.'

'But I wonder—have you had time to discuss this with your boyfriend?'

Alison was beginning to regret that she hadn't been honest with him from the start, yet she didn't see how she could back down now without making a fool of herself.

'I believe in making my own decisions,' she said.

Clint's eyes glinted. 'A modern relationship.'

'Yes, it is.'

'He doesn't mind, then?'

'Should he?' she asked abruptly.

'That's something only you can answer.' There was a look in his face that she could not define.

Alison pushed back her chair. 'I'm going to need some information, Mr Demaine. When exactly does camp start? And what is the best way of getting there?'

'I was just coming to that. How soon would you be free to leave here, Alison?'

'As soon as I'm needed.'

'How does tomorrow sound?'

Her head jerked up. *'Tomorrow?'* she echoed.

'Camp doesn't start till the beginning of the week, but you'd be doing me a real favour if you could travel down with me tomorrow. I just had word yesterday that the girl who takes care of the administrative side of things is going to be delayed a day or two, and I could do with some help setting things up.'

'Tomorrow...' Alison said again, slowly.

'I'd pay you for the extra days, of course. It's short notice, Alison, I know, but do you think you could possibly manage it?'

She stared at Clint, unaware that he wondered at the sudden light in her huge green eyes. He couldn't know that by going with him tomorrow, she would be getting away from the small village before the razzmatazz engagement party Edna's father was throwing for the young couple. Away from the hurt and the humiliation—for

Alison had fully intended going to the party—of having to watch Raymond and Edna publicly pledge their new-found love for each other.

As for her own father, Alison knew he would not mind her leaving the stables at such short notice, for Dad would be glad she was taking the first step towards an independent life of which he thoroughly approved. It wasn't even as if he would have to manage on his own. Lynn was always willing to help, as was Rob, a boy from the village, who grabbed every chance he could to work with the horses.

Clint was looking at her. 'Well, Alison, do you think you could make it?'

'Yes,' she said at last, 'I think I can.'

CHAPTER TWO

'DID I get you up too early?'

Alison turned from the window to smile at the extraordinarily attractive man at her side. 'Not at all.'

'Family didn't curse at being dragged out of bed at an ungodly hour to say goodbye?'

She laughed. 'Mom and Dad are up with the birds every morning. We're a farming family; the stables are just part of what we do.'

The first time I've heard her laugh, Clint thought. And then, I wish I could see her eyes. I wonder whether the sadness goes when she laughs.

'We've something in common,' he observed. 'I grew up on a farm too.'

Alison stared at him. 'Really, Mr Demaine?' Somehow she hadn't expected that.

'Yes, really. A sheep farm. And don't you think it's time you started calling me Clint? Things are pretty informal at Bushveld.'

'Clint . . .' The name had a strange kind of feel on her tongue.

'Have you always lived out in the country, Alison?' he asked.

'Always. It's the only life I know, and I love it.'

'The boyfriend's not of farming stock, I take it?'

Wary suddenly, Alison looked at him. 'Why do you ask?'

'Just drawing conclusions. I noticed he wasn't around to say goodbye to you.' It was said lightly enough.

Alison curled her nails into her palms. 'That's because Raymond and I...' She stopped.

Though she had decided she would tell him the truth, now she hesitated. Alison was not a girl given to lying, but yesterday, when she could have told Clint about Raymond, she had chosen not to do so. And today, perhaps, there was an advantage in continuing with the deception. She knew next to nothing about Clint Demaine. If he had any ideas about sex—and what man didn't try to make the most of whatever might be available?—then it was as well if he thought that she was off limits.

'Because we said our goodbyes last night.' Her voice was stiff.

'I see.'

'A *private* goodbye.'

'The best kind.' His face was turned forward to the road, so that Alison could not see his eyes.

'The very best kind,' she agreed firmly.

The Porsche had devoured another couple of miles when Clint threw out his next question.

'Are you engaged?'

'No...'

'Will you be?'

Talk about putting her on the spot!

After a moment, she said, 'Does it matter?'

'Something in your voice says, "and make of that what you will",' commented Clint.

'Yes, that's right,' she agreed.

'Which is what I have in mind.'

The outrageousness of the remark had her swinging round to him. Just for a second he took his eyes from the road, and she saw that they gleamed—a most unholy gleam.

Alison was suddenly intensely aware of Clint Demaine. The confines of the car dictated that she could only sit so far from him. Clint's legs, taut and tanned, his broad shoulders, his arms with their constant play of ligament and muscle, were just inches from her. She could not have said quite why, but the man had an inherent sexuality that made her nerve-ends feel raw.

Turning her head away from him, she said brightly, 'I really know very little about Bushveld Camp.'

'You do know that it's an adventure camp for children?'

He sounded amused that she had changed the subject, but she didn't care. 'I know that there's riding...'

'There's swimming too—canoeing, hiking, tennis, outdoor survival techniques.'

'Sounds like fun.'

'Yes, it's fun. Many of the kids come back year after year.'

'What happens if a family can't afford your fees?' she asked.

'That happens, of course, but no child has ever been turned away because of financial problems.'

She glanced at him, allowing herself to respect him for that.

'Do you live at Bushveld all year?' she queried.

'On and off during the camping weeks, and now and then when I want a break. Not as much as I'd like to, unfortunately, I'm afraid—my hotels keep me busy most of the year.'

'Hotels?' she exclaimed in surprise. 'You don't mean the Demaine chain?'

'You know them?'

'Of course! At least,' she amended, 'I know about them.'

The Demaine hotels were a burgeoning chain of luxury hotels, each one known for its high standards of comfort and efficiency. Wherever they were situated in the country, tourists came flocking.

'Do you actually own them?' she asked.

Clint laughed. 'Yes, I do. And I wish you wouldn't look so awed, Alison.'

'You can't fault me for that.' She looked at him with new interest. 'I don't understand, Mr Demaine—with all those hotels, where does the camp fit in?'

'It's the thing I love,' he explained. 'When I was a youngster, my happiest times were spent with my three brothers out-of-doors.'

'And so now you're giving other young people a similar opportunity?'

'Something like that,' he agreed.

'That's wonderful!'

'Thank you.' He paused a moment before asking, 'Is there anything else you'd like to know about the camp?'

Alison was caught by something in his tone. 'Do you mind me asking questions?'

'Not at all. In fact, I'd be very pleased if I thought you were really interested.'

'You think I'm not?'

'I think,' Clint said smoothly, 'that you try very hard to turn the subject away from yourself.'

She dug her nails deeper into her palms. 'That's absurd!' she muttered.

'Is it?'

'Yes, of course.'

'Then why are you so uptight whenever I mention your boyfriend?'

'Look, Mr Demaine, I don't want to talk about him...'

'Clint. And you're uptight again now. Every time I mention your boyfriend there's a kind of leave-that-subject-alone in your manner.'

'I'm a private person, Mr Demaine,' she said stiffly.

'Clint,' he insisted.

'Clint,' she complied in a choked voice.

'Private—and not very happy?'

Alison's head jerked up. Was he deliberately trying to hurt her? But the look in eyes that turned momentarily to meet hers was not malicious.

'I'm very happy,' she told him. 'Why shouldn't I be?'

'That's something you might tell me.'

'Even if I wasn't...happy...and I am!...that wouldn't concern you. You're just my employer.'

Only my employer.

'Anything that affects the well-being of my staff is my concern,' he said softly.

'Well, I am happy.' She made her voice as bright as she could. 'I wish you'd believe me.'

'I might if you'd relax.'

'I'm relaxed . . . Clint. And I really wish you wouldn't go on with this.'

Alison was shocked when he put his hand on her leg. Tight muscles jumped as liquid fire ran up her thigh to her groin. Recoiling, she pushed his hand away.

'Why did you do that?' she snapped furiously. In that moment he was not her employer; he was just a man—

a dangerously attractive man—who was beginning to get to her.

He laughed softly. 'Just proving to you that you're not relaxed at all.'

'What you just did could be taken as sexual harassment,' she said angrily.

'You know it wasn't.'

'I wonder!'

'You don't need to wonder. I wasn't out to offend you, Alison.'

'I don't go in for touching, Mr Demaine. You might as well know that,' she said firmly.

'You must lead a lonely existence,' he drawled. But she noticed that this time he let pass the formal use of his name.

'I'm not lonely,' she said stiffly. 'It's just that nobody touches me without my permission.'

'The exception being the boyfriend?'

When was the last time Raymond had touched her? Kissed her?

Firmly, she said, 'Exactly.'

For almost an hour after that there was silence—a charged kind of silence which began to get intensely on Alison's nerves after a while. She began to wonder how on earth she would get through the hours till they reached the camp.

And then, several miles further on, they saw the first placards advertising a country fair, and Clint asked, 'Would you like to look around?'

'Love to!' Just the idea of getting out of the car for a while spelled relief.

When Clint had nosed the Porsche between dusty jeeps and caravans, they made their way into the fairground.

Music blared through loudspeakers. There were crowds of people. Farmers, with floppy hats on their heads and *veldskoene* on their feet, inspected the livestock with practised eyes. Their wives, in jeans and checked shirts or light cotton dresses, engaged in animated conversation with friends they had not seen since the last get-together. Children swarmed everywhere.

'Will you know people here?' asked Clint, as they made their way between the rows of stalls.

'Maybe,' said Alison, 'though I shouldn't think so. I don't see any faces I recognise. We had a fair much closer to home about two months ago.'

'Did you have any part in it?'

'Did I! My sister Lynn and I sold six dozen jars of the best fig jam you ever tasted. And Mom won second prize for her chocolate cake.'

He laughed, the vital laugh that was beginning to sound familiar. 'Sounds as if you had a good time!'

She hadn't known about Raymond's two-timing then.

'A wonderful time.' She looked up at Clint. 'If I live till I'm a hundred, I'll never get tired of country fairs—the smells and the sounds and the people, the excitement. I love it all!'

'I can see that,' he smiled.

'Why are you smiling?' she asked, a little uncertainly.

'Because you're showing me a new side of yourself, Alison—vibrant, alive. I like you this way.'

Gold flecks warmed his eyes when he smiled, and his lips lifted in a way that was disturbingly sensuous. Alison stiffened as she tried to ignore his attractiveness.

Clint was saying, 'Do you know, it's ridiculous, but I can't remember the last time I was at a fair myself. You'll have to be my guide.' He cupped her elbow in his hand. His hand felt so big, the palm rough against her skin, the fingers folding over on to her arm. 'Lead on, fair damsel. I want to see it all.'

It was impossible to resist him when he was in this mood. Amazingly, she found herself laughing as they began to move through the crowd.

At a baked goods stall they stopped, and Clint bought some *melktert* which they broke in half and shared. When they'd finished it, they stopped again, this time to buy some *konfyt*. The sticky confection, made of glazed watermelon, was more difficult to break. Politely, Alison said she didn't really want any, but Clint would have none of that, and he insisted on holding it to her mouth until she bit off a piece. She was laughing again when he wanted her to have more, convinced that she would burst if she did.

Eventually they found themselves at the livestock, but they looked only casually at the cattle before moving on to the horses.

Leaning their arms on the whitewashed wood railing, they watched the horses being walked around a big paddock. Alison was all alertness now, inspecting horse after horse with the eye of one who did not mean to let too much time pass before she began buying some horses of her own.

'Look at that one.' She gestured towards a high-stepping horse. 'Isn't he super?'

'Certainly is,' Clint agreed, only to say a moment later, 'But look at that roan, Alison. See it, coming up on the right? Now there's a beauty if ever I saw one.'

Alison narrowed her eyes as she focused on the horse that was just coming up alongside them, step sure yet graceful, head proud and lovely, dark coat gleaming in the sun.

'Magnificent!' she said, awed. And then, with astonished respect, 'You understand horses, Clint.'

'I like to think I do.'

'That's one of the loveliest horses I've ever seen.' As Alison turned to Clint, her new-found respect led her to confide in him without thinking. 'The money I make at Bushveld Camp could never be enough to buy that horse. But I'm going to put it into a special account and keep it there till I have enough to buy one just like it.'

'Good lord!' exclaimed Clint.

'You don't approve?'

'I'm amazed, that's all.'

Alison laughed up at him, enjoying his confusion. 'Why?' she asked.

'I thought you might have your earnings earmarked for other things—trousseau, honeymoon, things like that.'

She managed to keep the smile on her face. 'And all the time I wanted it for a horse.'

'Mind telling me why?' His voice was unaccountably soft.

'I'm going to be starting my own stables.'

The surprised expression in Clint's eyes deepened. 'How does the boyfriend feel about that?'

'I told you,' her voice was light, 'I make my own decisions.'

After a moment, he said, 'So you're after acquiring your own stables?'

'That's right. As soon as I have enough money. I've worked with Dad for years, but I've always dreamed of a place of my own. I'll board horses for people who

can't put them up themselves, and I'll give lessons. I
want to organise gymkhanas, and...' She stopped.

When she went on, it was in a different tone. 'Why
are you looking at me like that, Clint?'

'You intrigue me,' he told her.

'I thought perhaps I was boring you.'

'Do you know, Alison,' dark brown eyes held her green
ones, defying them to move from his, 'I've a feeling you
have a great many qualities, most of which I've yet to
discover. But boringness could never be one of them.'

'Thank heavens for that!' She laughed up at him, then
turned her eyes back to the horses, but not before Clint
had seen that her cheeks were flushed with pleasure at
the compliment.

But a moment later the compliment was forgotten. A
nervous horse was coming their way, head jerking, gait
skittish, when Alison spotted a little boy climbing the
slats of the paddock fence. Little more than a toddler,
three years old at most, he got to the top of the fence,
balancing unsteadily as he waved his hands at the horse.

'Careful!' shouted Alison in alarm.

She lunged for the child, meaning to pull him back,
when he overbalanced, falling headlong into the
paddock, directly into the path of the horse.

Alison was levering herself frantically over the fence
when strong hands pulled her back, and in a second Clint
had vaulted into the paddock. He snatched the child from
the ground just as the front hooves of the horse were
about to smash down on it. And then he was back at
the fence, passing the little boy across to Alison

It had all happened so quickly that the horse's owner
had not had time to control his rearing steed. From start
to finish, the incident had lasted less than a minute.

Only now did reaction set in. The horse's owner, badly startled, and obviously thinking Clint and Alison were negligent parents, was cursing all three of them. The child, cradled in Alison's arms, began to cry. And then the mother rushed up, white and shaken, and took the child from Alison's arms.

'Thank you—oh, thank you!' She was crying as she turned to Clint. 'I just turned my head for a moment, and Bobby here ran away. I should have known better.'

'No harm done,' Clint said kindly.

'It's all my fault!' Tears streaming down her face, the woman hugged the child to her.

Alison touched her arm. 'These things happen. Look, you've had an awful shock. Why don't you go and get yourself a cup of tea? You might feel better then.'

'I'll go and find my husband first.' The woman turned to Clint. 'I don't know how to thank you.'

'You've thanked me already.' Clint ruffled the little boy's hair. 'Take it easy next time, cowboy.'

When the woman, still holding the little boy in her arms, had walked away, Alison said, 'That was quick thinking, Clint—and very brave.'

He smiled at her. 'I was no braver than you, Alison.'

'Me? I didn't do a thing!' she protested.

'You were going to. Have you forgotten that I stopped you from jumping into the paddock yourself?'

Wide-eyed, she stared at him. 'Yes, I had forgotten. Why did you stop me, Clint?'

The smile turned wicked. 'Put it down to masculine arrogance.'

She shook her head. 'No, it wasn't arrogance. But I could have done it—I'm used to horses and fences, Clint.'

'So am I,' he said easily.

After a long moment Alison said, 'You really did grow up on a farm, then?'

'Really. I thought that surprised you the first time I mentioned it. Why, I wonder?'

She had to think about it. 'Your image, I suppose. Your... your clothes, your car. All those hotels.'

He was so close to her that she could feel his laughter shaking his body. 'Trappings that all came much later. I didn't grow up owning hotels, Alison.'

After a moment she asked, 'What kind of sheep farm was it, Clint?'

'Merinos, mostly. Like you, I spent my youth on horseback—helping the men look for lost sheep, checking broken fences.'

They were still standing at the paddock, arms in front of them on the wooden rail, but now Clint shifted position, so that his arm was touching Alison's. A strong arm, deeply tanned, with the suggestion of hard muscle and sinew just beneath the skin.

Where his arm touched Alison's, her skin felt as if it was on fire. She wanted to remove herself from that touch, yet she didn't know how to do so without seeming childish in Clint's eyes.

She kept her eyes straight ahead of her. 'How long did you live on the sheep farm?' she asked him.

'Till I was twelve. My mother died then, and the heart seemed to go out of my father. Dad sold up, and we became city people after that.'

'That must have been hard for you.'

'It was at the time.' And then in a different tone, he said, 'Alison...'

'Yes?'

'This isn't touching.' His voice was soft. 'Not the kind of touching you were referring to in the car.'

Her head swung round at the words, but after a fevered moment she looked away from him again. 'I suppose you're right...it isn't,' she agreed quietly.

'Not that I wouldn't like to touch you in just that way.'

'Don't say that—please!'

'You're so awfully uptight,' he observed. 'I wish I knew why.'

'It's...nothing personal. I just don't go in for touching strangers, that's all. I already told you that.'

'I thought the last hour had taken us beyond being strangers.'

On a dry throat Alison said, 'I may be working for you for a little while, but basically we'll always be strangers, Clint.'

She didn't stop to wonder why his lips tightened at that. She was only conscious of a strange sadness deep inside her. She was relieved when he shifted his arm away from hers and said, 'Would you like to try out the roan, Alison?'

'Oh, yes!'

'All right, then, let's see what I can arrange.'

Clint strode away, lithe and loose-limbed, and as tall and tanned as any of the farmers. Alison watched him stop the man walking with the roan, and talk to him for a few moments. And then they were walking back towards her.

Minutes later Alison was in another paddock, astride the lovely horse. This was her world, the world where she felt secure and happy, no matter what. There was just the horse beneath her, and the wind stinging her cheeks and tugging at her hair.

In the veld she'd have ridden for hours. As it was, the ride couldn't last long. At last, reluctantly, she had to slow the horse to a gentle trot, and after that a walk.

Clint was right beside the horse as Alison made to dismount, his hands reaching for her waist.

'I haven't been helped off a horse in years,' she protested.

He laughed at her. 'Doesn't mean you can't be helped this time! Enjoy the ride, Alison?'

Her eyes were great and green and shining. 'That's just the most marvellous horse!' she told him eagerly.

'You looked marvellous riding it.'

It was the compliment that brought home to her the fact that he was still holding her—a loose hold, his hands just touching her waist. There was no reason at all why the touch had the feeling of an embrace.

She took a step backwards, away from those big hands, and Clint did nothing to stop her. Instead he said, very softly, 'Do you know how beautiful you are?'

'Shouldn't we be moving on?' Her voice was jerky.

'In a moment.'

Reaching out, he pushed a strand of wayward hair behind her ear. Alison tried to ignore the excitement that flamed suddenly inside her.

'Clint . . .' she began.

'That wasn't touching, either, Alison. Nothing you could object to. You know that.'

'It must be getting late,' she said, taking another step away from him.

'Does your boyfriend tell you every day that you're beautiful, Alison?'

'Stop this, Clint!'

'I'd never stop telling you so if you were my girl.' His voice was low and husky, as caressing as his touch had been.

'But I'm not your girl.'

'No, you're not, are you?' His hand went to her hair again, smoothing it from her forehead this time. 'I know one thing: if you *were* my girl I'd never have permitted you to go away with another man.'

'I haven't gone away with another man,' she gritted. 'I've taken a job. I'm travelling to the camp with you—that's all there is to it. You know that as well as I do.'

'I'd want you near me all the time if you were mine.' He was so close to her that his breath was warm on her cheek.

For the merest moment she caught herself wondering what it would be like to be constantly near a man like Clint Demaine. And then she caught the thought and pushed it firmly away from her.

'You talk of belonging, but I can never belong to anyone.' Her voice was harsh now. 'Not in the way you seem to be implying. That kind of relationship isn't for me.'

'Does that mean you're not in love, Alison?'

Her head jerked sharply. 'My private life doesn't concern you, Clint. And I really wish you'd stop talking this way, you can see it upsets me.'

'I'm not sure why. You must be used to having men tell you that you're lovely.'

When was the last time Raymond had said she was lovely? A long time ago, she realised now.

'It's getting late, Clint,' she said.

He didn't answer immediately. He stood for a long time just looking down at her. Her cheeks felt warm, her lips were trembling, and she did not need a mirror to tell her that her eyes were distraught. And Clint was just standing there, looking at her, and she knew he was taking all of it in.

Suddenly he smiled, the devil-may-care smile that was beginning to do strange things to her system. She would have to learn to harden herself against that smile.

'It's going to be a good summer, Alison,' he remarked.

'I hope so.'

'I know so.'

With one of those unexpected movements he reached for her hand. He held it only briefly, and because she decided to take the gesture as one of friendship, she did not pull away from him.

But long after his hand had left hers she could still feel the warmth of it burning her skin.

It was mid-afternoon when they reached Big Willow Farm, where Clint had some business to discuss with the owner, Don Anderson.

They'd been leaving the fair when Clint had stopped to phone the farm from a public booth. When he'd told Don that he'd be later than he'd first thought, and that he was bringing someone with him, Don's wife had insisted that they spend the night at the farm.

The Andersons were at the car by the time Clint and Alison got out—Jenny, a pretty young woman with fair hair and very obviously pregnant, padding down the steps of the big stone veranda, and Don, very tall, almost as tall as Clint, jumping from a jeep with two labradors at his heels.

'Don! Jenny, love.' Clint shook the man's hand, then hugged the woman to him. 'Good to see you both.' He turned to Alison, who hung back a little shyly. 'This is Alison Lenox. She's driving up to Bushveld Camp with me. Alison, I want you to meet my very good friends, Jenny and Don Anderson.'

After the first niceties were over, Don's approving eyes swept the racy lines of the Porsche. 'Nifty car! New since the last time you were here.' He grinned at Clint. 'But then I've always admired your taste in cars—as well as in women.' The last was said with a smile at Alison.

The words had Alison drawing in her breath. Involuntarily, she took a step backwards.

Her reaction was not lost on Jenny, who threw her an apologetic look before saying, 'Now, Don...'

'It's not the first compliment Alison has received today.' Clint threw a wicked grin at Alison.

She managed a smile in return. 'It's not, is it?'

But the smile was difficult. So she was not the first female Clint had brought to Big Willow Farm. *Why on earth did that matter to her?*

She was about to tell the Andersons that she was not one of Clint's women, when Clint threw a teasing look in the direction of Jenny's middle. 'Seems to me something got in my way when I hugged you, Jenny. You're looking great, honey.'

'Great in more ways than one.' Jenny was flushed with pleasure. 'I know you and Don have things to discuss, but let's eat something first.'

Alison followed Jenny into the spacious farmhouse kitchen, where copper pots hung from the walls and pot-plants stood in happy profusion on the windowsills. On one side of the room, long strips of *biltong* hung to dry from the rafters. In a corner stood an ancient creamer, a reminder of the days when women had had to make their own butter.

'This makes me think of home,' Alison said to Jenny. 'My mother would love your kitchen.'

She carried the tea-tray to the table, while Jenny took an apple tart out of the oven and put it down beside a dish of warm scones.

They were drinking their tea when Clint turned the conversation back to Jenny. 'So this man of yours has made you a mother.'

'An expectant mother. We'd like you to be godfather, Clint.'

'I'll be happy to. Especially if the baby's a girl, and even half as beautiful as her mother.'

Jenny mock-grimaced down at her stomach. 'Call this beautiful?'

Clint was not the man to leave the comment at that. Beneath the benevolent eye of her husband, he began to flirt with Jenny. Bemused, Alison watched the other girl sparkle. Although she could not help but know that most of what Clint said was just provocative nonsense, Jenny was opening up to Clint like a flower opening to the sun.

Glancing at Don, Alison was surprised to see him beaming. Don, she realised wonderingly, was seeing the carefree girl his wife had been before the onset of chores and pregnancy. Obviously he was secure enough not to mind that another man's attention had wrought the transformation.

Well, it was fine for Don to be unconcerned. As for Alison, she had been warned. She would have to make sure she was on her guard against Clint Demaine, who had doubtless been charming women—and discarding them the moment the next challenge appeared—since he was old enough to shave. With his brand of sex appeal and dynamic good looks that would have been so easy for him.

The meal finished, the men left the farmhouse. Alison remained behind to help Jenny.

They had almost finished washing up when Jenny said, 'Clint is quite a man, isn't he?'

'Yes, he is,' Alison agreed, and proceeded to tell her hostess how Clint had vaulted the paddock fence to save the little boy.

'It's what I'd expect from him.' Jenny smiled. 'I bet he was modest about it afterwards.'

'Yes, he was.'

'Tough as they come, that's Clint.' And with a mischievous look at Alison, 'Sexy, too. Not that that's something I need tell you!'

Inside Alison, something tightened. 'Look, Jenny, there's something you should know—I don't happen to be one of Clint's women.'

Jenny looked startled. 'You *were* offended by Don's remark.'

'No, of course I wasn't! But I thought I'd set the record straight. I have a job at Bushveld Camp—that's the only reason I'm travelling with Clint.'

'That remark about Clint's women—it was silly, but Don didn't mean anything, you know. He was just joking.'

But he *had* meant it; Alison was sure of it.

Jenny was looking unhappy. 'I hope you didn't mind me flirting with Clint.'

'Good heavens, no!' exclaimed Alison. 'Why on earth would I?'

'It doesn't mean anything, either—Clint knows that. Don does, too.'

'So do I,' said Alison. 'In any case, it really doesn't concern me.'

Except that, for some reason, it *did* concern her. And the person Alison was angry with was not Jenny, but herself.

'I'm glad you're not upset,' Jenny said. 'I love my Don very dearly, and I wouldn't trade him for the world. And I'm so excited about the baby. But right now the pregnancy's beginning to wear me down, and I suppose... Well, if truth be told, I was feeling a bit envious of you.'

'Envious of *me*?' Alison asked incredulously.

'You're so carefree—no responsibilities to tie you down. Going off with Clint, having fun.'

'I'm going to be *working* for Clint,' Alison said carefully.

'You'll be having fun at the same time.'

'Yes, I will. I enjoy kids and horses.'

'*Fun with Clint* was what I meant,' explained Jenny.

'You're quite wrong,' Alison assured her.

'Not that the others won't try to get their share of him,' Jenny went on, as if she had not heard the protest. 'Especially the camp director, Virginia. She runs the camp for Clint, and I think she rather fancies him. I heard that they'd spent quite a bit of time together last year. Still, the fact that you'll be alone with him before the others arrive gives you an edge.'

Alison's lips were so tight that her jaw ached. 'You don't understand. I don't want to be alone with Clint.'

Jenny looked surprised. 'Don would say it isn't any of my business, but will you take a well-meant word from someone who's just beginning to learn what it is to be tied down? Don't turn your back on fun, Alison.'

'Fun!' Alison made a harsh sound in her throat. 'I'm not interested in having fun. At least, not if by fun you mean a man.'

Jenny's eyes were compassionate. 'I get the feeling you've been hurt,' she said quietly.

After a moment Alison said, 'Yes.'

Jenny began to stack the dishes in the kitchen cupboard. For a minute or two the domestic clatter of dishes and cutlery was the only sound in the kitchen. At length, without turning, Jenny said quietly, 'Clint has been hurt, too.'

The words caught Alison by surprise. 'Someone let him down? I find that hard to believe.'

'Much worse than that. Clint was married. His wife died.'

Alison drew in her breath. 'Good lord! I'm sorry, I had no idea...'

'He doesn't talk about it very often.'

'Did it happen recently?' Alison would have been hard put to it to identify the strange emotion she was feeling.

Jenny frowned. 'Quite a long time ago, actually—eight or nine years. Clint was very young at the time, about twenty-three, I suppose.'

'Did you know her, Jenny?' Alison asked.

'Linda? No. I only met Clint after I married Don three years ago.'

'And he's never remarried?'

'No.'

'There must have been women, though. You mentioned the camp director, Virginia...'

'I don't know how many women there've been, Alison.
Don really was joking when he made that remark.'

'If...if Clint doesn't talk about his wife, why have
you told me?' Alison asked.

'I just thought it was something you might like to
know.' Jenny treated her to a direct look. 'I like you. I
like Clint.'

And then, before Alison could make anything of that,
Jenny looked at her watch. 'I'm exhausted. I never
dreamed pregnancy could be so tiring! Would you mind
very much if I went and had a nap before dinner?'

Alison smiled at her. 'I wish you would. What can I
prepare for you in the meantime?'

'Not a thing, but thanks all the same. Don will organise a *braaivleis*, and the salads are in the fridge. Look,
do you have your swimming costume handy?'

'Yes, I do.'

'The pool is at the bottom of the garden. And if you
don't feel like swimming, there's a whole stack of maga-
zines on the veranda. Just make yourself at home.'

The two men were nowhere to be seen as Alison walked
to the pool. Despite the gathering shadows, it was still
very hot. The veld was silent. Even the slight wind that
had blown much of the day had stilled. In the distance
the *mielie* fields stretched towards the horizon and
beyond. A *piet-my-vrou* called to its mate from its perch
in an acacia, and from the farmhouse behind her Alison
heard the barking of the labradors.

The water was wonderful—cool enough to be re-
freshing, yet still warm enough to relax. Alison swam
until she grew tired, then she rolled over on to her back
and floated with her eyes closed.

Eyes that snapped open in alarm when a hand touched her back, then widened when they looked up into a laughing face.

'What on earth——!' she gasped.

She tried to stand, to twist away from Clint, but his arm had folded around her, holding her weightless body in such a way that her feet could not have touched bottom.

'No, Clint—no! What do you think you're doing?'

'Answering a mermaid's call.'

'I'm not a mermaid!' she protested.

'You could have fooled me. Lying there, so sleek and beautiful, with your hair drifting behind you on the water, what else could you be?'

She tried to move away from him, but he moved quicker than she did. His other arm was holding her too now, resting just below her breast. She could feel every one of his fingers on her skin, imparting sensations that were quite frightening. She tried once more to stand, but it was too deep where they were, and instead of touching ground her feet brushed his legs. Suddenly, even her toes tingled with life.

'I'm not a mermaid, Clint. Nor was I calling you.' Her voice was jerky.

'Is that really what you would have me believe?' He was laughing again. His eyes were very dark, but the gold flecks lit them, warmed them. His eyelashes were long and thick.

'Of course.' Her heart was beating hard inside her.

'I don't think you mean that. You must have known the picture you made. Your swimming costume so low...just here...'

His fingers touched the swell of her breasts, and her breath jerked in a harsh gasp.

'Stop it, Clint...' She didn't know if the words made it past her lips, or if they were stuck in her dry throat.

If he heard her, he gave no sign. 'Shapely legs seducing me on the water.'

'You have to stop this! You really do,' she said faintly.

His only answer was to hold her tighter against him as he bent his head all at once and began to kiss her. A slow kiss, tantalising, and so erotic that something wild and unexpected stirred deep inside her, a raw and primitive ache, a sensation Alison did not want to acknowledge, though she seemed helpless to do anything about it.

For at least a minute he went on kissing her, his tongue playing at the corners of her lips, trying to coax a way between them. And then suddenly sanity returned, and with it some of her strength. Balling her fists, she pushed them hard against his chest.

His head lifted, but his arms remained around her. His hair was wet, clinging to his head, as he grinned down at her, white teeth flashing against the wet tan. A pirate—erotic, marauding, sexy.

'Why did you do that?' Eyes blazing, she flung the words at him.

'I wanted to,' he shrugged.

'And do you always do everything you want?'

Dark eyes glinted. 'Whenever possible.'

She tried again to stand, but once again her feet made contact only with his legs.

'I told you how I feel about touching. Clint, how could you?'

'You're making such a big deal of it. I thought we shared a lovely day, Alison. A kiss seemed like a good way to end it.'

'I hated it!' she snapped.

'Did you really?' he asked very softly. 'I sensed your body telling me a different story.'

Was it possible that he had sensed her excitement? 'You'll never have me.'

'I'm not sure about that,' he drawled.

'Have you forgotten that I have a boyfriend?'

'I haven't forgotten that he allowed you to come away with me.'

'I told you—I make my own choices.'

'I believe he could have stopped you.' Cupping her face with one hand, he tilted her head a little away from him. 'You're not wearing a ring, Alison.'

'Rings don't mean a thing,' she shrugged.

Not true. They did. They meant love, commitment, a lifetime together. Very soon now Edna would be wearing Raymond's ring on her left hand.

'This isn't the moment to debate rings, Alison.' Clint's face was inches from hers, his voice husky. 'We're here alone together, you and I, a man and a woman. I want you so badly. I believe we want each other.'

Alison trembled. As they swayed together in the water, she could feel the evidence of his desire against her, and she realised that in his own fashion he was probably being restrained.

She pushed at him. 'All I want is for you to let me go, Clint. I can't take any more of this, I really can't!'

His arms were hard around her, like bands of steel imprisoning her vulnerable body. Alison made herself go limp in his embrace. And then suddenly his arms loosened, and she was free.

With trembling limbs she swam to the edge of the pool. Gripping the stone wall with her hands, she turned her head and looked back at Clint.

'Don't try that again,' she warned. 'Ever. I won't stand for it!'

CHAPTER THREE

IT WAS the day of Raymond and Edna's engagement party. The day Alison had never dreamed could ever happen had arrived. Tonight Raymond and Edna would officially tell the world that they loved each other enough to spend their lives together.

Overriding Alison's emotions of anger and betrayal was a sense of total unreality. Going all the way back to her childhood, she could not remember a time in her life when she and Raymond had not been together. Which was why it was so very difficult to think of him making his life with another woman. There was a finality about this day which made her very sad.

Trying her best to push Raymond and Edna from her mind, Alison showered and dressed. Clint was nowhere to be seen when she entered the camp kitchen. The sparkling mountain air made her constantly hungry, but this morning, her third day at Bushveld, she was not in the mood for food. After pouring herself a cup of coffee, she made her way to the office.

A little grimly, she looked at the heap of files on her desk. At least she would be too busy to think about Raymond.

For several hours she worked steadily, and then her interest was suddenly sparked by a file that was different from the rest.

Alison was frowning as she put down Timmy Roscoe's file. Why was Timmy coming to Bushveld Camp? Why an adventure camp for this particular child? Would he be able to participate in the camp activities? Did he need special treatment?

Pushing aside the file, she stretched her cramped back and legs. She'd been at the desk all afternoon, doing the paperwork which Patricia, the girl who had been delayed, would normally have done. Unaccustomed activity for Alison, who was used to the physical work entailed in running a stable.

The desk was near the open window. From where she sat Alison could not see very much of the mountains— the Drakensberg, whose majesty surpassed anything she had ever imagined—but she could see the velvet green of the lower slopes. High on a barren cliff, above the green, a bird swooped, then soared out of sight. She smiled as she watched two lizards chase each other on a sunny rock near the window.

And then a tall figure strode purposefully into view. By the time Clint appeared in the office, the smile had vanished from Alison's face.

He grinned at her from the doorway. 'Still at it?'

'Still at it.'

'Patricia will be duly grateful.'

'I hope so.'

He came to stand by her chair. 'I think it's time for a break.'

He was all male, utterly and overwhelmingly male. The strong lines of his face were echoed in the powerful proportions of his body. His shoulders and chest were broad, his hips narrow. Accompanying the strength was that constant aura of sexuality which was as much a part of him as his long, tanned limbs.

In his presence, Alison felt alarmingly vulnerable. 'I think I'll go on for a while,' she said.

'Glutton for hard work, are you?'

There was something in his smile that was infinitely disturbing, so that she found she had to look away from him. 'Not exactly.'

'Or are you running away from me?'

'Good heavens, what's that supposed to mean?' She sat back, pretending astonishment.

'We both know you've been doing your best to avoid me since we arrived here,' Clint said calmly.

'I've been working,' she shrugged.

'That's a lame excuse, Alison.'

A pulse throbbed in her throat. 'Don't you ever stop?'

Clint laughed softly. 'Have dinner with me tonight. We'll go up to the hotel.'

Alison didn't have to consider the invitation. 'Thanks, but I don't think so.'

'Why not?'

'I . . . I'm not really in the mood.'

He laughed again, a husky laugh which many another woman might have found seductive. 'My guess is that you're still thinking of our kiss in the pool.'

She lifted her chin at him. 'And if I am?'

'I'd say you were making too much of it. It was just a kiss, Alison.'

'There's something you're forgetting, Clint.'

'The boyfriend, I suppose,' he said drily.

Today, the lie was especially painful. But necessary, she reminded herself. 'Yes.'

Clint's jaw tightened. 'How we always get back to him! I find that strange, since he hasn't bothered to phone you once since we've been here.'

The blade twisted a little further in the wound. 'That doesn't mean anything.'

'I'd phone you every hour if you were my girl, Alison.'

'To check up on me? He's not the jealous kind.'

'And you, Alison—what kind are you?'

'I really don't think that can be of any interest to you.'

She tensed as Clint caught her wrist in his fingers. 'Wrong,' he said. 'I'm interested in everything about you.' He began a slow, stroking movement with his thumb, a movement that was so sensuous that Alison felt her pulse begin to race beneath the long fingers.

'There's not much to know about me.' Her voice was choked. 'Look, Clint, about...'

'*Do* you get jealous?'

'Of course not. Clint, about this entry here...'

'If you're never jealous, then perhaps you're not really serious about that man you left behind.'

The stroking grew more sensuous by the moment. Alison did not know how much longer she could bear it.

'I wish you wouldn't keep on about him.' In vain, she tried to pull her wrist out of the grip of the wicked fingers. 'And stop doing that! You know how I feel about touching.'

'*Will* you have dinner with me?'

Raymond and Edna would be having a good time tonight.

'Well, all right, thank you,' Alison said.

'Good.' Despite her somewhat ungracious acceptance, Clint sounded remarkably pleased. 'Can you be ready to go around eight?'

*   *   *

Heads turned as they walked into the dining-room of the hotel. Alison was certain that all the looks were directed at Clint, who was easily the most attractive man in the place. What she did not realise was how many male eyes were turned her way.

She was looking very pretty in a narrow-waisted, rose-pink dress which emphasised the slim curves of her figure and enhanced the colour of a heart-shaped face. Narrow straps revealed a slim neck and smoothly tanned arms and shoulders, while an antique silver pendant on a thin silver chain nestled between her breasts. Lynn had persuaded Alison to pack the dress and pendant—with Alison arguing that she would have no use for pretty things in a children's holiday camp. The auburn hair, which she normally wore tied back in a snood hung loose and shining to her shoulders, and her lovely green eyes were luminous beneath a dusting of green shadow.

'This must be one of your hotels,' she remarked, having noted the special deference with which Clint was treated by everyone, from the receptionist in the lobby to the haughty maître d' and the waiter who came to take their order.

'Yes, it is. This was the first one. The others—there are ten of them around the country—came later.'

'So this hotel must have special meaning for you?'

'It has. One day, I hope, you'll see the others.'

Politely Alison said, 'I don't do much travelling.'

'That can be remedied.' There was something enigmatic in the look he gave her.

Alison made herself smile smoothly back at him. 'Oh, I doubt it. I'll be far too busy to think of travelling once I get started on my stables.'

'When do you think that will be?'

'I don't have a date. So much depends on the money I can come up with. But I'm going to start with the planning as soon as I get back from camp.'

'You still haven't told me what the boyfriend thinks of your plans.'

He had a way of riling her with Raymond. 'I told you the first day that I do what *I* want!' she snapped.

'I just wonder about his feelings,' Clint said mildly. 'Does he approve?'

'Why shouldn't he approve?' Alison's tone was abrupt.

'No reason at all.' Dark eyes lingered for a long moment on a small, flushed face and trembling lips. 'What shall we drink to, Alison?'

Her reply was brisk. 'The success of the camp.'

'Do you know what I'd really like to drink to?' he asked softly.

'What?' Her questioning look was open and unguarded.

'I'd like to drink to the day I make love to you.'

Alison jerked in her seat. Then she shoved the wine away from her, so abruptly that a few drops stained the white cloth. 'That's outrageous!'

Clint gave a shout of laughter, drawing the eyes of people at nearby tables. 'Are you always so prim? It must drive that boyfriend of yours crazy.'

She looked at him through pain-filled eyes. 'Clint, please...'

Something of her emotion must have got through to him, for the laughter suddenly left his face. When he spoke again, it was in a different tone.

'That was just my way of telling you that I find you very beautiful—and desirable.' His hand went across the table to touch one of hers, very briefly. 'I'm sorry if you

were offended. We'll drink to the camp, if that's what
you prefer.'

They raised their glasses, and said 'To the camp,' but
there was a look in Clint's eyes that made Alison shift
in her seat.

She was relieved when the first course was served, a
delicately flavoured rack of lamb, with new potatoes done
in a parsley butter sauce and mushrooms marinated in
wine sauce.

'I was working on Timmy Roscoe's file this morning,'
she told Clint, glad to be turning the subject away from
herself. 'I see he was injured in a motor accident.'

'Right. It occurred very soon after he'd been enrolled
at camp. Poor little kid—he was travelling with his
parents when their car was hit by a drunken driver.
They're lucky to all be alive.'

'But his parents are still in hospital?'

'They were quite badly hurt, yes. Timmy was lucky
to get away with a broken leg. He's staying with relatives
now.'

'The plaster cast has been removed, hasn't it?'

'Yes, it came off recently.'

'Poor little mite, he's only ten,' Alison said sym-
pathetically. 'He must be feeling so confused and
frightened. I wonder how many camp activities he'll be
able to participate in?'

'Most of them. He may feel a bit fragile for a while,
but his leg is basically all right now. Timmy's aunt and
uncle considered withdrawing him from the camp, but
his parents still wanted him to come. Fortunately,
Virginia—our camp director—will know how to handle
him. She knows a lot about children.'

'Really?'

'She's studied a fair bit of child psychology, and she does a good job of running the camp for me.'

It was said with such confidence in Virginia. Virginia, who had probably been something more than friends with Clint, if Alison had understood Jenny correctly. Alison had a sudden picture of Virginia—clever, beautiful, sophisticated, tremendously sexy.

'It doesn't take psychology to help a hurt child,' she said.

'It helps.'

'I would think hugs and kisses are more important than psychology,' Alison said thoughtfully.

Clint looked taken aback for a moment. 'You've got something there. But don't underrate Virginia. She's very competent.'

'I'm sure she is,' she agreed.

'She's been leading the camp for years. And that's very important to me, because the hotels quite often take me away from Bushveld.'

Alison played with the food on her plate. 'It must be a relief to know you have competent staff.'

'It is,' Clint agreed. 'But I didn't bring you here to talk about Timmy and Virginia. If you've finished your lamb, I want to dance with you.'

Alison hesitated, wanting to refuse him. If she meant to remain detached from all men, the last thing she should be doing was to dance with this one particular, too attractive man.

He was watching her. 'You do dance, don't you?'

Raymond and Edna would be dancing tonight, celebrating their future. It was ridiculous for Alison to sit around and be miserable. Have fun, Jenny had said.

So she smiled at Clint across the table, her eyes glowing in the candlelight. 'I adore dancing,' she admitted.

The band was enthusiastic. The music was quick and loud, the dances lively. Best of all, they were dances that did not require touching. It came as no surprise to Alison to find that Clint was lithe on his feet. As she laughed at him across the safe space that separated them, she couldn't think when last she'd had such a good time.

The band stopped playing for a while, and Alison and Clint went back to their table for strawberries and cream and more wine. When the music started again, Clint cocked an eye in the direction of the dance-floor, and this time Alison needed no persuading.

And then the mood of the music changed. It became slower, more mellow—golden oldies meant for closeness, for dreaming. For the first time, Clint held Alison in his arms while they danced. Somewhere deep inside her a voice sounded a warning, but the good food and all the wine had had an effect on her, so that the warning was no more than a murmur.

She made no protest when Clint's lips touched her hair, and he drew her against him. She actually found herself enjoying the sensuous movements of the long male body against hers. With the wine dulling her mind, she only knew that it felt good to be close to Clint.

Shock hit her when the band began to play 'In the Mood'. *Their* song—hers and Raymond's. And then Clint begun to hum the tune against her ear, just as Raymond used to do.

She pushed against Clint, who said, 'Relax,' and went on humming as he drew her closer against him. Alison was distraught now. It didn't matter that it was Clint who was humming and not Raymond. She only knew that she couldn't bear it—not tonight of all nights.

So upset was she that she didn't stop to wonder what Clint would think as she twisted out of his arms and hurried from the dance-floor. There was only one thought in her mind—she had to be alone.

Clint came after her. 'Wait!' he was saying as she grabbed her bag, but she didn't hear him. She was only intent on getting out of the place.

She didn't see the curious glances of the other guests as she rushed headlong from the dining-room and through the lobby of the hotel. She didn't notice the darkness outside. She didn't even notice the isolation as she began to run, awkwardly on her high heels, in the direction of the camp some five miles down the road.

When the lights of a car came on her from behind, she shrank into the darkness at the side of the road.

The car shrieked to a halt. A door opened, banged shut, then someone bore down on Alison—an intensely angry man, who didn't seem in the least affected by the sight of the girl quivering like a small wounded animal in the bushes.

'You little fool!' he shouted. 'Get in the car!'

She put out her hands to ward him off. 'No...'

'This minute!'

'I...I'd rather walk.'

'Are you coming out of there? Or do I get you out by force?'

The menace in Clint's tone was not lost on Alison. He would drag her to the car if she didn't co-operate— that was no idle threat.

'I'll come by myself...' she began.

He took her arm as she emerged from the bushes, and propelled her towards the car. There was nothing gentle in the way he bundled her in and closed the door. As the car took the road to the camp at a spanking speed, Alison huddled against her door, as far as she could get from six feet two inches of very angry man.

'Clint . . .' she said once, tentatively.

'Later,' he advised abruptly, and she was wise enough to leave it at that.

The moment they reached camp, Alison opened the car door, thinking to make a quick getaway to her cabin while Clint was parking the Porsche. But this time he had the wisdom of foresight. In the time it took her to walk three steps away from the car, he had caught up with her, and seized her arm.

'Clint, please . . .'

'Skip it,' he ordered, and marched her to her cabin.

She had only one hope left—a slight one. While Clint was driving she had taken her key from her bag; it was in her hand now. The moment they reached the cabin she opened the door and tried to walk quickly through it. But any hope she'd had of closing the door in his face vanished as he inserted his foot through the doorway.

'No, you don't!' Clint was in the cabin too now. He flicked on the light, then advanced towards Alison. He looked stern and dangerous.

'Leave me, Clint.' Her head was up, her tone as firm as she could possibly make it, as she tried to hide her fear. 'Please leave me.'

'Sit down.'

She decided to stand her ground. 'I'm very tired.'

'Not that tired. Sit down, I said!'

Sensing that Clint Demaine in a temper would be a dangerous man to contend with, Alison decided to comply. She sat down on the little two-seater settee by the window. It was either that or the bed.

Clint didn't sit. He just stood there, looking down at her, and his expression did not fill her with joy.

'What the heck was that all about?' he demanded.

She wetted her lips with her tongue. 'I'm sorry.'

'Sorry?' He spat out the word. 'Sorry? My God, Alison, you behave like a child. And then you think you can brush the whole thing aside by saying you're sorry!'

'But I am—I really am.'

She put her hands in front of her eyes to hide the tears that she was trying so hard to hold back.

'What got into you? I thought we were having a good time.'

'We were,' she muttered.

'That you were relaxed for once.'

'I was.'

'Did I hold you too tight? Was that what frightened you into behaving like an outraged virgin?'

She shook her head. Her throat was so full of tears that it was hard to speak.

Gripping her shoulders, Clint gave her a little shake. 'You have to tell me, Alison. You owe me that much.'

'Raymond...' She swallowed hard on the tears. 'Raymond liked ''In the Mood'', even though it's an oldie. Mom and Dad have the record at home. We...we used to dance to it, Raymond and I, and he...he would hum the tune in my ear—just as you did.'

Clint's lips tightened. His face was thunderous. 'Good lord, is that what this drama is all about? ''In the Mood'' brought on such a bout of homesickness for the wretched

Raymond that you had to go and behave like a second-rate actress?'

'It's not like that...'

But he was too angry to hear her out. 'Alison Lenox—the independent woman who didn't give a damn for what her man thought when it came to taking a job. Who just went ahead and made her own decisions without even talking to him.'

'I know you're angry, but you don't understand...'

'Too right, I don't! Do you know how I felt on that dance-floor, Alison? All those people watching as you ran from my arms and out of the hotel—as if I'd done something thoroughly indecent!'

'Oh, God, I'm so sorry. I didn't think about that. I don't blame you for being angry, but you see...'

'All you thought about was how much you were missing Raymond. If you love him so much that the mere sound of another man humming your song throws you into histrionics, then you should have refused my offer, no matter how much you want to buy a horse. You love him, he loves you. Why on earth did you agree to come away with me?'

In a choked voice, Alison said, 'Raymond doesn't love me.'

Clint took a step backwards. He looked stunned.

After a moment he said, 'You've lost me, Alison. Somehow I thought Raymond was the love of your life.'

'I thought so, too.' Her throat was so raw that it felt like sandpaper.

'Perhaps you'd better explain.' His voice was a fraction softer now.

'Raymond left me. We'd had an argument...'

'People do have arguments. You'll make it up.'

'No, we won't.' She looked up at him. Tears hovered on her lashes, but her eyes were steady. 'You see, there's someone else. Her name is Edna, and they're getting married.'

'Good heavens!' And then, 'The man must have been an absolute fool to let you go.'

'Do you really think so?'

'I wouldn't say so if I didn't.'

There was something in the way he said the words that made Alison feel better. For the first time since she'd run away from him on the dance-floor she didn't feel like crying her eyes out.

'The engagement party is tonight,' she added.

After a long moment Clint said, 'So that's why you were so upset.'

'It's been on my mind all day.'

'No wonder! And yet you agreed to come to the hotel with me.'

'I thought I'd feel better if I was out and having a good time. For a while, I did feel better. I really was enjoying myself. And then . . .'

'Then I hummed that darn tune in your ear.'

'There's no way you could have known.' She looked at him hopefully. 'Do you . . . do you understand why I behaved so stupidly?'

'Understand?' In a second he was by her side, folding his long body beside her into the settee. 'I'd be an insensitive clod if I didn't understand. What I don't understand is why you didn't tell me the truth.'

Awkwardly she said, 'There were reasons.'

Mercifully, he seemed prepared to leave it at that. There were no more questions as his arm went around her and his hand tightened on her shoulder. Alison did not push him away.

It felt so *good* to have some human contact, to feel as if someone cared. It didn't matter that sympathy was probably as much as Clint was offering. She didn't want more from him than that. And although she was trying very hard to be self-sufficient in every possible way, to-night of all nights sympathy was something she could afford to accept.

'Did you come away with me because of Raymond?' Clint asked at length.

'No.' She turned in the circle of his arms and looked up at him. His eyes were dark and alert. 'I wasn't running away.'

'I didn't think you'd be the type to do that.'

'I'm not!' She sounded suddenly fierce. 'Oh, I won't pretend I'm not glad to be away from all the excitement going on at this moment—I am. But I meant what I said about getting my own stables. It's something I've always wanted. The money I earn at Bushveld really will go towards a horse. *That's* why I took the job.'

'In which case,' he said drily, 'I wonder why your first reaction was to refuse me.'

Alison moved her eyes from his. She didn't see how she could tell him that the reason she'd refused him was because he was too attractive.

'I . . . I suppose I wasn't thinking properly. Does it matter, Clint?'

He laughed softly. 'All that matters is that you did come, and that you're here with me now.'

His other arm went around her, and now he was folding her against his chest. She did not protest when he began to kiss her. His kisses were gentle, and tonight her defences were down. Stronger than all her resolutions was her desire to feel beautiful, to feel *wanted*.

Then the kisses deepened, becoming hungrier, more passionate. Demanding a response.

Reality returned quite suddenly. Horrified at what she had allowed Clint to do, Alison stiffened. But he did not seem to notice. One of his hands slid beneath her dress to the soft bare swell of her breasts.

The breath jerked harshly in her throat, and then she was pushing him away from her.

Clint's head lifted. 'What's wrong?'

'You know what's wrong,' she said through tight lips. 'I don't want this.'

'Everything's changed, Alison.'

'Nothing has changed for me.'

He was sitting a little away from her now. His eyes were dark and speculative. 'You don't owe Raymond loyalty any longer.'

'It's not a question of loyalty.' Her throat felt raw. 'You don't understand, Clint. I don't intend to replace Raymond—not with you, not with anyone.'

She heard his hissing intake of breath. 'You're still feeling hurt.'

'But thinking clearly.'

'Alison...' He was reaching for her again.

But this time she eluded him. 'Go, Clint. Please go.'

For a long moment they sat quite still, looking at each other.

'We will make love—one day,' Clint said at last.

'No.'

'When you're ready for it.'

'I'll never be ready.' Alison was beginning to tremble.

His expression changed suddenly. There was a sparkle

in his eyes, and his lips lifted at the corners. '"Never" is one word I've always refused to recognise.'

The trembling was becoming worse. 'I need to be alone now, Clint.'

'I'm going.' He smiled at her as he got to his feet. 'Sleep well, Alison.'

The door closed behind him, and she took a long, shuddering breath. Sleep well ... She'd be lucky if she slept at all.

CHAPTER FOUR

ALISON was busy with paperwork again the next morning when Clint appeared in the office. He looked so very attractive as he smiled at her from the doorway that Alison was powerless to control a strange stirring within her.

'Working again?'

'Just earning my salary.' She was uneasy with him after what had happened the night before, but she tried to hide her feelings with a smile.

'I'd like you to do something quite different this morning,' he told her.

'Oh?'

'The saddles in the stables could do with a good polish. They're in a sorry state.'

Eyes widening with surprise, she looked at the pile of files in front of her. 'I still have quite a bit to do here,' she said.

'This will keep,' he said easily.

'But, Clint, the counsellors arrive tomorrow, and the campers two days after that.'

'Patricia will be back by then, and she'll deal with what's left.' He grinned at her in pretend disbelief. 'Are you telling me you mind working in the stables?'

The words had her on her feet in a second. 'It's what I *adore*!'

Five minutes later she was perched on a low stool in the stables with a pile of saddles, a jar of polish and some cloths on the floor at her feet. With a sigh of pleasure, she took a saddle and began to work on it.

This was Alison's world—the whinnying of the horses, the clopping of hooves, the smell of fresh straw. The feel of saddle-leather between her hands, the dimness of the stables in contrast to the glare of sun-baked rock outside. This was the world she loved.

She straightened in surprise when Clint appeared. She was even more surprised when he drew up a stool beside her and took a saddle from the pile.

'I can manage these on my own,' she protested.

'Four hands make for faster work than two. Have you any objection to my helping you?' There was a smile in his voice.

After a moment, she said, 'No... It isn't necessary, though.'

'Perhaps not,' he agreed, but he remained where he was.

For a while they worked in silence, Alison continuing to polish the saddle on her lap as if nothing had changed. But for her something had changed. Till then she had enjoyed the smells and sounds of the stables, now she was conscious only of Clint.

He was buffing the polish on a saddle when he broke the silence. 'This is where Bushveld Camp started,' he told her.

She looked up. The light was too dim to make out the expression in his eyes, but she was caught by something in his tone.

'These stables?'

'This used to be a fishing shack. It was much smaller, of course, most of it was added later. But part of the original structure is still standing.'

He fell silent again, and Alison, sensing that he had begun to tell her something important, did not speak either.

At length he went on. 'I was married once, did you know?'

'Jenny told me...'

He doesn't talk about his marriage often, Jenny had said. Alison could not have said why she felt suddenly tense.

'Then she must have told you that Linda died, nine years ago, in a senseless accident. Afterwards...a couple of weeks afterwards...I came up here.'

'Here?' Alison whispered.

'I was crazy with grief. And ridden with guilt, because I'd allowed her to drive on a stormy night, when I should have made her stay at home.'

'Were...were you alone?'

'It was the way I wanted it. I had to be alone, to grieve, to think—to make some sense of things.' Clint put down the saddle and looked at her. 'Years ago, my father used to bring my brothers and me up here to fish. It was the place where I used to be happiest. When tragedy struck, I came back.'

'You must have loved Linda very much,' Alison said softly.

'Yes, I loved her. She was small and sweet and pretty, and I always felt I had to protect her. That was what made the guilt all the worse.'

'You weren't to blame.'

'You couldn't have convinced me of that then.' Clint picked up the saddle and resumed his polishing. 'The first months after Linda's death were very rough. But somehow I survived. And it was partly this place that did it—the mountains, the stream, the wild beauty of the veld.'

'It *is* beautiful here,' she agreed. 'Even more beautiful than I'd expected.'

'The most beautiful place in the world for me. When I decided to start the camp, this was the natural place to build it. And the hotel up the road was the first of the chain.'

Bravely, Alison said, 'Jenny said you don't often talk about Linda.'

'She's right about that. Even Don doesn't know that I came here. Or what this place did for me.'

Silence fell between them once more. The swishing of the polishing cloths and the grunting of a horse in a nearby stall were the only sounds in the stables. Alison polished fiercely, almost as if her life depended on it.

At length, it was her turn to break the silence. 'Why did you tell me, Clint?'

'I wanted to.'

'It was more than that. You brought me here on purpose to tell me. I could have gone on working in the office, the saddles could have waited.'

'I had to tell you I was sorry.' Clint's voice was soft.

'Sorry?' Her head jerked.

'I've behaved very badly since we met—teasing you constantly about Raymond.'

'You couldn't have known,' she said painfully.

'Maybe not, but there was something odd about the relationship all along. The fact that he wasn't around to say goodbye to you when we left. He didn't phone. And you were so uptight every time I mentioned him.'

'You couldn't have known,' she said again.

Without warning, he reached out a hand to cover one of hers. The contact shocked her. Where it touched her, his skin was so warm and alive, stirring a longing deep inside her that she tried very hard not to acknowledge. Beneath his fingers her hand stiffened.

At her reaction, Clint's hand left hers. 'At any rate, I was insensitive. I'm sorry.'

Alison took a breath. 'Thank you.'

'Feel like talking about it?'

'Heavens, no! I don't want to bore you.' The words came out too quickly.

'I told you once before that you could never do that. And it helps to talk. Trite, I know, but true.'

She looked at him thoughtfully. It had been almost impossible to talk to her family; they were too close to her, to Raymond, too cut up about the whole thing. And so terribly sorry for her. They didn't seem to understand that their pity only made things worse.

'I can't remember a time when Raymond wasn't part of my life,' she said at length. 'We were toddlers together, Clint. I mean, we shared the same toys and played in the same sandpit. All through school we were in the same classes. We were best friends. We did everything together.'

'Sounds like brother and sister,' Clint observed drily.

'In a way, Raymond was the brother I never had,' she acknowledged.

'You don't marry a brother, Alison.'

'I know what you're trying to say. But things changed. At some point in high school we became boyfriend and girlfriend. It was taken for granted we would get married one day.'

'Taken for granted by whom?' Clint asked quietly.

'Our parents. Ourselves.'

'It doesn't sound very exciting, Alison.'

'It wasn't exciting,' she conceded. 'It was...' she searched for a word, 'comfortable. I knew—I *thought* I knew—that Raymond and I would always be there for each other. I was wrong...' Her voice quivered.

A moment passed, then Clint said, 'Last night you talked about an argument.'

'A very silly argument, yes.'

'Why didn't the two of you sort out your differences?'

'At first I was too proud. Raymond was always the first to make things up, and I thought I'd wait for him again this time. Afterwards...well, I tried to make the first move when I saw he wasn't going to do it. But it was too late by then.'

'He'd already taken up with Edna?' Clint asked disbelievingly.

'Thinking back, I realise now that things hadn't been all that good for a while before the argument. And Edna—I know now that Raymond was already seeing her. Considering the size of the village, it's amazing I didn't know, but I didn't. It seems they went out of their way to keep their meetings secret.'

'I think you said Edna was the boss's daughter.' Clint's tone was noncommittal.

'And Raymond is ambitious, yes. But I believe there's more to it. I think he loves Edna. I really don't believe he could be so ambitious as to want to marry her just because her father can do great things for him.' She put her hand over her eyes. 'No, I can't believe it's that.

'The worst of it was the way I found out.' Her voice was very low now, it was the only way she could keep herself from crying. 'I decided to go to Raymond's house, to try and patch things up. And I...I found them together. They were lying on a sofa...kissing.'

'My God!' he muttered.

'Raymond was terribly embarrassed, of course. But he told me he loved Edna and that he was going to marry her. For a while I couldn't believe it. There was this great emptiness inside me.'

'That's something I know all about.'

'Yes, you would. But Clint, I felt so let down, disillusioned. If I couldn't trust Raymond, there was nobody I could trust.'

'Not every man is like Raymond,' Clint said quietly.

'That's something I'll never know.'

His voice changed. 'I hope you don't really mean that.'

'I told you last night that I didn't intend to find a replacement for Raymond, and I meant it,' Alison insisted.

Clint reached for her hand again. 'You think that now because you're still hurt. I believe the time will come when you will love again, Alison.'

'I won't let it happen. In fact, I'll make quite sure it doesn't.' She drew her hand away from his. 'When I found out about Edna I wanted to die. I was so jealous of her, Clint, it was awful!'

'A normal reaction, I'd say.'

'Maybe so, but I don't want to experience it again. Yesterday you asked me if I was the jealous kind. I'm never going to be jealous again, Clint. You can only be jealous if you love someone, and I don't intend to let myself love again.'

'What about loneliness?'

'I won't be lonely. I'll have my stables and my horses, all the things I like best. I'll never have to wonder whether a man is interested in me because he loves me, or because I happen to be the diversion of the moment.'

She looked at him steadily in the dim light. 'That's why I didn't tell you the truth about Raymond. I didn't want you thinking I was fair game just because there was no longer a man in the picture.'

'Your opinion of me is flattering,' he said drily.

'It's not personal, Clint. It would have been the same with any man.'

'I see.'

'Anyway, perhaps now you can understand why I don't want to be touched?'

'You're a lovely woman, Alison. I know that you're warm and caring, and I sense that you've a great capacity for love. Are you really going to deny yourself a normal life?' He sounded troubled.

'That part of my life is over,' she said firmly. 'I'm not likely to change my mind.'

She was surprised when Clint asked her to have dinner with him at the hotel again that evening.

'After what happened last night? Aren't you embarrassed to be seen with me?' she queried.

'I don't get embarrassed that easily,' he said cheerfully. 'The counsellors arrive tomorrow, Alison. Let's have one lovely evening together before this place becomes a madhouse. I won't make a pass at you, I promise.'

And, in fact, it really was a lovely evening. There was none of the strain of yesterday; tonight they talked and laughed with the easy enjoyment of two people who had become friends.

The food was delicious—a succulent fish this time, caught in the cold, fresh waters of the mountains. Once again Clint ordered wine, a sparkling Riesling that came from vineyards much further south than the Drakensberg.

Time passed quickly as they talked about music and films and books they had both read, and Alison was amazed to find how much she was enjoying herself. The conversation was eager and spirited, for their opinions differed widely.

One film in particular was the subject of keen discussion. It was a movie they had both enjoyed, though each had seen it in a different light. Clint saw Miranda, the heroine, as a charming schemer; to Alison she was a helpless victim of circumstances. A good ten minutes were spent discussing plot and character, with neither Clint nor Alison willing to compromise their views, while each acknowledged that the points the other made were good ones.

Alison was laughing when they finally agreed to call a truce. 'Not that we settled that one.'

'But we had a good time disagreeing, didn't we?' Clint's eyes sparkled at her over the candlelight.

'Oh, we did! A marvellous time. I remember coming out of that movie with Raymond, and feeling I wanted to talk about it.'

'Didn't you?'

Alison tightened, but only briefly. 'Well, no... There would have been no point to it, really. We'd have had the same opinion.'

'How could you know that without testing it?' Clint was watching her.

'Because we always thought the same way.'

'About everything?'

'Most things. Our likes, our dislikes, everything was the same. We always knew what the other was thinking.' She paused a moment. 'Oh, don't look at me like that, Clint. There's nothing wrong with two people being so similar.'

'Except that the similarity could get boring eventually.'

'You'll be saying next that we didn't really love each other,' she said crossly.

'Did you?' he asked quietly.

'Of course we did!' she came back, a little too quickly. 'I can't remember a time when I didn't love Raymond. I thought you understood that.'

'I believe that you loved him.' His voice was very soft now. 'But were you *in love* with him?'

She stared at him. In the glow of the candlelight, her eyes were smudged with shock. Clint's eyes held hers, not wavering even when her lips began to tremble.

Alison was the first to shift her gaze away. 'I feel like dancing,' she said.

They went to the dance-floor, and Clint took her in his arms; neither of them referred to the fact that Alison had not answered his question. They danced till the band took a break, and then they went back to their table and had dessert and coffee and more wine, and the discussion turned to horses. The one topic they didn't touch on again was Raymond.

It was late when they got back to the camp. At the door of Alison's cabin they stopped, and she looked up at Clint.

'You're safe,' he smiled down at her. 'I'm not going to force my way in.'

'Just as well.' She was smiling back at him. Yet, inside her, belying the words and the smile, was a most contradictory frisson of disappointment.

'Not that I wouldn't like to,' he said lightly. 'I'm determined to live in hope, Alison.'

'It's getting late, Clint. Thank you for a very lovely evening.'

'I'm the one to thank you,' he said softly.

He reached towards her, cupped her face in those large hands of his, and kissed her. It was a gentle kiss, and it lasted just a few seconds.

Without a word, he released her then, and disappeared into the fragrant darkness.

Alison closed the door. She did not switch on the light, but went instead to the window. For a few minutes she just stood there, resting her hot face against the cool glass pane, and trying to calm a mind that was surprisingly agitated.

It was a few minutes before she felt calm enough to close the curtains and get ready for bed. But in the moments before she finally slept a question burned in her mind. The question which Clint had asked her, and which she had not answered.

'I believe you loved Raymond,' he had said. 'But were you *in love* with him?'

The camp counsellors arrived a day later. Clint drove the camp van to the station, some ten miles away, to pick them up. They piled out of the van half an hour later, laughing, vocal, still catching up on the news that had taken place in the last year, all wearing jeans and T-shirts, and dragging an assortment of cases and totebags behind them.

All of them were young, Alison saw, as they were introduced. Early twenties, about the same as her own age of twenty-two. Gary and Brian, who would be supervising the boys, as well as organising canoeing and rafting. Mary, Wendy and Laurie, who would be looking after the girls, in addition to organising various sporting activities. Patricia, the girl who looked after the office work, had arrived too, apologising for her delay, and thanking Alison for having helped Clint out in her place.

Almost immediately Alison knew that if she was to have a special friend at the camp it would be Mary. Red curls flying, guitar strung across her shoulder, mischievous smile lighting up a merry face, it was Mary who said to Alison, 'Hello! Clint said we're neighbours. Do you mind the dulcet sounds of a guitar at all hours of the night?'

Alison laughed. 'Just as long as they're dulcet!' She'd been wondering what it would be like to be the new member of a group which had worked together a few years. Now she knew that she need not have worried.

'The fair Virginia made her appearance already?' Mary asked.

'Not yet.'

'She will, never fear.'

Virginia made her appearance an hour later in a fancy little red sports car, apparently new since the previous year, and which had Brian and Gary drooling. But Virginia barely acknowledged the envy of the young male counsellors. As she left the car, she had eyes only for one person.

'Clint!' She went straight to him, lifting her arms and her mouth for his kiss.

An embrace which a cheerful Clint did nothing to discourage, Alison noted grimly.

'You look wonderful!' Virginia was enthusing.

'You're looking pretty good yourself,' he grinned down at her.

She *did* look good—stunning, in fact. Tall, and with a superb figure, Virginia was a beautiful woman. With her sleek, blonde hair parted in the middle and resting on either side of her forehead in classic waves, she could easily have been a model. She was older than the other staffers, late twenties, Alison guessed, and unlike the casual jeans of the others she wore an emerald trouser suit that looked as if it had been lifted straight from the pages of *Vogue*.

'Does she always dress like that?' Alison asked Mary softly.

'Not when she's working. Then she goes in for safari suits, very tailored, very expensive, always stylish. There's no competing with her.'

Mary was right, Alison decided. It would be a remarkable man who would not be fascinated by Virginia.

She found herself having to try surprisingly hard to force a smile when Clint made the introductions.

'I'm very pleased to meet you, Alison. I hope you'll enjoy working at Bushveld.' Virginia's voice was low and husky, as sexy as her appearance.

'Thank you, Virginia, I'm sure I will.'

'Clint tells me you came down with him a few days ago.'

'Yes. There was quite a bit of paperwork to be done.'

'He kept you working all the time, did he?' This was said with a flirtatious look at Clint.

'Not all the time,' Alison said smoothly.

Virginia's blue eyes regarded her coldly. Then the camp director turned to Clint, and now her mouth was curved in a charming smile. 'You should have let me know. I would have come to help you if I'd known there was a problem.'

Later in the day a meeting was held in the games room. Clint officially welcomed the counsellors and made a short speech that was laced with good humour and friendly informality.

Then Virginia took over. The camp director's words were strictly to the point: a short run-through of the different camp activities, a list of objectives which Virginia expected both campers and counsellors to achieve. Everything precise, well thought out, well organised.

She addressed herself to each counsellor in turn, outlining his or her duties. When she came to Alison, her words were crisper, her voice cooler.

She doesn't like me, Alison realised. I wonder why. She can't possibly think that I'm competition for her.

Only when Virginia addressed Clint did her manner change. A deepening huskiness came into her voice when she spoke to him. Flirtatiousness was in her smile.

Alison watched Virginia and Clint standing together at the front of the room. There was an ease between them that spoke of long familiarity. Even if Jenny had not told her about Virginia, Alison would have guessed that they knew each other well.

Well—and so what? It really didn't concern her one way or another, she told herself. How could it, when she herself had no emotional interest in Clint?

CHAPTER FIVE

AT LAST the campers arrived: close on seventy of them, girls and boys, ranging in age from nine years to sixteen. They came with knapsacks and sleeping-bags and tennis racquets, some carrying fishing-rods. There were the 'oldies', the ones who had attended camp in previous years, who whooped when they saw old friends and were raring to embark on the summer's activities. And then there were the first-time campers. These were easy to spot, for they stood back, looking awkward and shy, and a little fearful at leaving home for the first time.

For the counsellors, there was lots to do—campers to be welcomed, registers to check, health cards to file, children to be sorted in groups, and directed to their cabins.

Confusion might have reigned, yet under Virginia's expert supervision all went smoothly. The camp director was remarkable. However hectic things became, she never grew flustered, and she always remained looking cool and beautiful.

It was late afternoon when a car bearing the last child arrived. A little boy got out of the car, then huddled against it, as if he expected some awful thing to happen to him. Looking younger than his ten years, he was waif-like and very pale, with huge eyes dominating his small face.

Timmy Roscoe. Alison recognised him immediately. Even if she hadn't been expecting him, she would have known who he was.

She went quickly to him. 'You must be Timmy,' she said gently.

The big eyes looked at her. 'Yes.'

'We've been expecting you. My name is Alison.' She looked up at the tall man next to him. 'And you must be Timmy's uncle.'

'Joe Roscoe, yes.' He was young and harassed-looking. Alison, who had been through Timmy's file more than once, knew that Joe's wife was in the last stages of pregnancy. Taking their little nephew into their home to convalesce while his parents were still in hospital after the accident had not been easy for them.

She gave the man her warm smile. 'You won't have to worry about Timmy, Mr Roscoe. We'll look after him.' Bending to the little boy, she gave him a hug. 'You're going to have a super time here, Timmy.'

He regarded her thoughtfully. Then, as if he'd decided to trust her, he gave a tentative smile. Her heart going out to him, Alison hugged him again.

She was about to say something more when an icy voice intervened. 'Thank you, Alison, I'll take care of things now.'

Alison looked up into Virginia's unsmiling face. Something tightened inside her, but she just said gently, 'See you later, Timmy.'

Clint arrived at that moment, and shook Joe Roscoe's hand. And then Clint and Virginia conferred with Timmy's uncle, while Alison, not quite knowing what to do, stood to one side.

At length it was time for Mr Roscoe to go. Timmy stood in one spot, watching the car until it was out of sight. He looked totally bereft.

'Time to go to your cabin, Timmy,' Virginia told him.

'OK.' Obediently he bent to pick up his suitcase.

Alison, knowing how recently the plaster cast had been removed from his leg, thought the case looked a bit too heavy for the frail child.

'I'll carry that,' she offered, moving to take the case from his hand.

But she hadn't gone two steps when Virginia stopped her. 'Timmy will carry his own case, Alison.'

Alison stared at the camp director, outraged. 'It's heavy!' she protested.

'All campers carry their own belongings.'

But Timmy wasn't 'all campers'. He was a little boy who was still recovering from a nasty accident.

Alison cast a look of appeal at Clint. 'Surely in this instance, Clint...'

Clint gave Alison a brief look which she did not understand. Then he smiled at Timmy and said, quite gently, 'Do you think you can manage the case?'

The boy nodded.

'Well, that's fine, then,' said Virginia. 'Gary there— see the counsellor in the green shirt?—he'll show you the way to your cabin.'

When Timmy, carrying his case, had gone off with Gary, Alison looked from Clint to Virginia. Her eyes were blazing. 'I don't believe what just happened! Why would it have been so wrong for me to carry Timmy's case?'

'Timmy Roscoe is to be treated like any other camper,' said Virginia coolly. 'The last thing he needs is pity.'

'Pity! Good lord, I wasn't showing him pity—just a bit of compassion!'

'Our opinions differ on that.' Virginia's tone was crisp. 'But whatever your opinion—and I'm sure you agree with me on this, Clint—I expect you to support my directions, Alison.'

Support? You cold bitch! The words sprang to Alison's tongue, but she saw Clint's warning glance, and clamped her lips.

'Alison has already shown that she has the interests of the camp at heart, Virginia,' Clint said quietly.

But that wasn't enough for Alison. Clint should have taken her side instead of trying to keep the peace, she thought mutinously. She saw him looking at her, but she refused to meet his eyes.

Anger churned inside her as she made her way to the stables—an anger that did not lessen when she began to groom the horses.

She decided to go for a ride before supper. It was sunset, and the sky was awash with brilliant shades of crimson and gold. The sun had left the lower slopes of the mountains, but the high peaks were bathed in a translucent radiance. A widow-bird dragged its heavy black tail across the scrub, and a tiny gazelle peeped out of a thicket at the cantering horse. It was all so beautiful, yet it did nothing to improve her mood. By the time she got back to the stables, Alison felt no better about what had happened with Timmy.

It was quite late in the evening when she eventually made her way to Timmy's cabin. Just inside the doorway she stopped. It was silent in the dark cabin. There was no sign of movement from the six bunks.

And then, just as she was about to leave, Alison caught the sound of muffled sobbing. In an instant she was beside the last bunk.

'Timmy?'

The sobbing stopped briefly, then resumed, more quietly this time, in a way that was even more heart-rending than before.

'Timmy...' She tugged gently at the top of the sleeping-bag which he had pulled over his head.

No response.

'Timmy, darling, what is it?'

Timmy's body shook with his weeping—an even quieter weeping now.

Alison sat down on the bunk and gathered him in her arms. 'It's all right, darling,' she soothed, as she stroked his damp hair and cheeks. 'It's all right.'

He did not respond. She didn't expect him to. She just continued to talk to him quietly.

'You're upset about your parents, aren't you? They're getting better, darling. They'll be out of hospital soon, and you'll be going home to them.'

Still Timmy said nothing, but slowly, very slowly, the pathetic shuddering began to lessen.

'You're going to have a good time at camp,' Alison told him. 'You're going to swim and play all sorts of games. There's a lovely lake, did you know that? And a big games room with a ping-pong table. There are horses for you to ride, and some nights we'll have a camp-fire and sit around roasting marshmallows and singing songs.'

There was a different feel to the little body in her arms. She knew he was listening. She tried to look at him in the darkness. 'Do you think you'll like that?'

A weepy sniff, then Timmy said, 'I suppose so.'

'And when your mum and dad get back home, think how much you'll have to tell them.'

Another shudder. 'I want them now.'

'I know, Timmy.'

'I miss them so much.'

'Yes, darling, I know. But you'll have a good time at camp, and think how quickly the time will pass.'

Timmy was silent. After a while Alison said, 'Do you think you'll be able to sleep now?'

'I'll try...'

'You do that. And listen, Timmy, if ever you need anything, or if something bothers you, you can always come to me.'

And blow Virginia, and what she might say to that!

Alison was walking away from Timmy's bunk when a figure moved out of the darkness. Letting out a startled gasp, she took a hasty step backwards.

'Hush,' he whispered.

'Clint!' she exclaimed.

He put a hand on her arm. 'We'll talk outside.'

'You gave me a fright,' she accused, when they'd left the cabin.

'Sorry about that.' She heard laughter in his voice.

'What were you doing in the cabin?' she demanded.

'Let's go for a walk, Alison. We can talk about it while we walk.'

'I don't think we have anything to talk about,' she protested, trying hard to ignore the burning sensation his hand produced on her arm.

'You know that's not true. Besides, we haven't been alone together since our dinner at the hotel, and I've missed that.'

Alison wanted to refuse him. But the way he added, 'Please,' so softly, so persuasively, seemed to leave her no alternative but to give in.

Side by side they walked through the deserted camp grounds. And then they had left the compound, and Clint reached for Alison's hand.

'I really have missed you,' he told her.

Stupid, treacherous heart, that it should leap at the words.

Voice firm, she said, 'We were going to talk.'

'All I want is to make love to you.'

Her hand jerked in his, but when she tried to pull away from him, he threaded his fingers through hers.

'You did say we'd talk,' Alison accused through lips that were suddenly dry. 'Was that just an excuse you invented to get me alone?'

He was so close to her that she could actually feel his laughter. 'Partly.' And then, more seriously, 'Yes, I do know we have to talk.'

Trying very hard to ignore the unsettling sensations his closeness was provoking inside her, Alison said, 'Why didn't you stand up for me this afternoon?'

'I couldn't do that—I hoped you'd understand.'

'No, Clint, I didn't! I still don't.' She turned her head, trying to see his eyes in the darkness. 'Why would it have been so wrong for me to carry Timmy's case? You read his files, you know what he's been through.'

'Yes, I know.'

'Then why?'

'I couldn't go against Virginia.'

She was suddenly very angry. 'Why not?'

'Because she's the camp director, and it would have been bad for camp morale.'

'But Virginia was wrong, Clint. That case was too heavy for Timmy.'

'I agree,' he said. 'She was wrong.'

'Then why didn't you say so? Because she's beautiful and sophisticated?'

Clint was quiet for just a moment. Then he said, 'I just told you—because she's the camp director. I know you don't think that's reason enough, Alison, but it is. Virginia runs this camp for me. She was wrong about Timmy, but she's generally good at what she does, and as much as I can I have to let her make decisions. You have to understand, Alison—I can't be here all the time. I'm involved with the hotels, sometimes I have to be away for weeks at a time. I depend on Virginia to keep things going without me.'

'But in this one instance, couldn't you have disagreed with her?'

'If it were just a case of one instance, but it isn't. There are times when I don't agree with Virginia—her handling of Timmy, for example—but I can't undermine her authority. Especially not in front of others. If I did, the camp would soon become a shambles.'

'I see,' she said, subdued. And then, 'Do you go away very often?'

'Often enough.'

I'll miss you. The thought was as shocking as it was involuntary.

For a while they walked in silence. It was very beautiful in the mountains at night. The air was cool and spicy with the scent of wild mimosa. Only a slim crescent moon hung in the sky, but a million stars shed enough light for Clint and Alison to see where they were going.

Against the starry sky the mountains were bulky, ebony shapes.

The path was narrow, and their linked hands brought them close together, so that their bodies touched as they walked.

'Why did you go to Timmy's cabin, Clint?' Alison asked at length.

'Same reason you did—to see if Timmy was OK.'

'You realised he'd be unhappy?'

'I thought he might be.'

Alison was silent a moment. Then she asked, 'How long had you been there when I saw you?'

'Long enough. I saw the way you comforted Timmy.'

She was caught by something in his voice. 'Anyone would have done it.'

'You'll make a wonderful mother some day, Alison,' he said quietly.

She tensed. 'I'll never be a mother.'

'You don't know that.'

'I do!' she said brittly. 'You know how I feel about men. I'll never get married.'

'You might change your mind.' It was said so oddly, that her heart pounded suddenly in her chest.

'I'll never change it,' she said, very firmly indeed.

Clint stopped and turned to her. He was still holding her hand, and now his other hand went to her face, the long fingers tracing a slow path around her lips.

'I told you once before that "never" is a word I don't have in my vocabulary.' His voice was low and seductive.

Her heart was pounding so hard now that she felt sure he must hear it. 'It's time to go back.' She was trembling.

He laughed softly, inflaming emotions that were already raw. 'In a moment.'

'No—I want to go now,' she whispered.

But his arms went around her, quite gently, as if he was determined not to frighten her. For a long moment he held her trembling body against him. One hand went to her hair, his fingers stroking it, threading through it, before coming to rest on the nape of her neck. She could feel his long body against hers, his shoulders and his chest and his thighs, so hard and strong that she became very conscious of her own soft femininity.

A minute passed, and then his hand moved to her throat, to her chin, tilted her head. Dimly, Alison understood that she should be pushing him away, but her brain seemed totally incapable of sending the correct messages to her body. There were feelings flooding her, sensations that were quite unlike anything she had ever experienced, so that she couldn't have pushed him away if she had tried—which she didn't.

His head came down then, and he was kissing her. Unlike the kiss in the swimming pool, this kiss made no demands. It was a tender kiss, yet so tantalisingly sweet that it was, in its way, almost more erotic than if it had been passionate.

Something primeval and utterly primitive stirred deep inside Alison, so that she yearned to put her arms around Clint's neck and bring him closer to her, to return his kisses with all the intensity that was in her. Her hands reached for his shoulders, and just for a moment her fingers gripped his shirt.

And then, miraculously, she realised what was happening to her. Her hands dropped to his chest, clenched, and now she was trying to push herself away from him.

'No...' she protested.

He lifted his head to look down at her. 'Let yourself enjoy it,' he said huskily.

'No! Oh, God, you shouldn't have started this, Clint. You had no right to!'

'Why not? You were never in love with Raymond, you know that now.'

'Maybe not.' Her lips were shaking, and there were tears in her throat.

'Then let me kiss you.'

He drew her towards him again, and now his kisses were more passionate. His tongue was at her lips, tracing the shape of them, trying to push them apart. A part of Alison wanted nothing more than to respond to him. But it was the very fierceness of her longing that gave her the strength to resist him this time.

Clint took a step back as she pushed against him. 'This is silly, Alison.'

'No, it's not! Don't you understand yet, Clint? This isn't for me.'

'You're wrong.' His breathing was ragged. 'There's warmth and passion in you, Alison. I've seen the way you ride the horses, the way you were with Timmy. You've so much life in you, so much to give.'

'Not as far as sex is concerned!'

'You only think so because you've been hurt.'

'And I don't intend to be hurt again. I want to go back to camp. Please!'

But he was still holding her. 'It was just a kiss, Alison.'

Her legs were still weak from that kiss, and deep inside her was the aching longing that had not grown less for all her brave words.

She twisted out of his arms. 'Let's go.'

'Don't turn your back on life, Alison.'

She made herself look up at him. 'I'm only turning my back on the kind of life *you* seem to think is right for me. I'll be totally happy running my own stables, Clint, doing the things I want to do. I don't *need* men in my life.'

'What about love?'

'That's an illusion.' Her voice was short.

'And the joy of human contact?'

Her body throbbed with the need to be touched by him—to be held in his arms, to kiss and be kissed. She wanted him so much that her trembling body felt on fire.

It was very hard to conceal her trembling. 'I don't need it,' she insisted.

Clint stroked her cheek, and she had to summon all her strength not to go back in to his arms. 'You're wrong. Everyone needs it, Alison. For a long time after Linda died I thought differently, but eventually I understood that I was wrong.'

She looked away from him. 'I must be different.'

'I don't believe that. I felt you respond—I know I didn't imagine it. I believe that for a moment you really wanted to take things further.'

Alison was badly rattled now. 'You really are dead wrong!' she flung at him. 'I'm going back to camp, Clint. Are you coming with me, or do I go alone?'

They walked down the path together—silently now, for there was nothing left to talk about.

The lights of the camp grounds were in sight when Clint slowed his step.

'I'm not giving up on you, Alison. I won't rush you, I promise. When you're ready, you'll let me make love to you.'

'You'll wait a long time,' she said tensely.

'I'll wait until you're ready.' And this time there was a smile in his voice.

Two days later, Clint was called away to clear up a problem at one of the hotels. Alison told herself she was relieved he was gone.

Life at Bushveld Camp had settled into a pleasant routine. Alison spent most of her day with the horses. In the mornings she led the older campers on trail-rides through the foothills. In the afternoons the younger children would come to the paddock. They were not ready for trail-riding, but Alison taught them a little about horses, and let them ride, one at a time, along an easy path, while she walked beside the horse and held the rein.

Timmy was at the stables whenever he could get away from his other activities—which annoyed Virginia, who felt he should be swimming or canoeing or playing volley-ball with the other children in his group. But, after the first day, Alison quietly went her own way. Timmy was still feeling unsettled, and Alison was the one person with whom he felt comfortable. And so she allowed the little boy to help her groom the horses, and she gave him more than his share of rides.

Timmy was denied only one pleasure. More than anything he wanted to go on a trail-ride, but on this point Virginia was adamant. Timmy was too young, his group did not participate in trail-riding. That was that.

Evenings were fun. After the *braaivleis* there was almost always a camp-fire. Mary, who had indeed become Alison's closest friend at Bushveld, would bring out her guitar, and while marshmallows sizzled on the flames, children and counsellors joined in a sing-song.

Alison's only irritant was Virginia; she liked the camp director even less now than on the first day. Now and then she wondered why it was that she wanted to strangle Virginia every time she saw her. And yet the only reason that presented itself was one she could not—would not—accept.

She tried very hard to stay out of Virginia's way, and when that was not possible she made it a point to be sweetly reasonable with her. She made it a point never to clash with her.

And yet clash they eventually did.

Timmy's parents had arranged to send him a tuckbox. Alison, who was in charge of mail the day it arrived, gave it to him. Timmy's eyes glowed, his little face was radiant when he realised from whom the present had come. Over and over he ran his hands over the box, his whole being alive with a happiness which Alison had not seen in him since the day he had arrived at camp. He walked away, still holding the unopened box.

About half an hour later there was the sound of a scuffle in Timmy's cabin. Alison took no notice at first, but when she heard screaming she hurried to investigate. For a moment she stood quite still in the doorway. The floor was a mass of squirming, noisy bodies, so that for the first few seconds she was not sure what was happening.

And then she saw Timmy, in the centre of the trouble—a frantic Timmy, eyes wild, one fist flying, the other hand trying hard to hold something to his body while another child tried to snatch it away, and yet another was pummelling his head.

Alison, always protective of Timmy, dived into the fray without thinking. All she knew was that Timmy was in a situation which he could not handle alone.

'Leave him alone!' she yelled, pulling the boys away from Timmy. 'Leave him, you little bullies!'

Startled faces jerked around as two boys found themselves in her grip. They were trying to wriggle away from her when someone demanded, 'What's the reason for this disorderliness?'

Virginia had entered the scene. Immaculate as always, her expression one of cool distaste—an expression that seemed directed solely at Alison.

Bit by bit, told in excited voices, the story unfolded. Timmy's cabin-mates had found him opening his tuckbox. They'd wanted a share, and Timmy had refused. He wanted to keep the box intact a while before making a start on it, he said. So they had decided to take what they wanted by force.

'I want to see you in my office,' Virginia said to Alison when order was at last restored.

One look at the camp director's face was sufficient to tell Alison that she was in for a lecture. And a lecture was what she received.

'This cannot go on.' Virginia crossed one elegant safari-suited leg across the other.

Alison stared at her. Her face was still flushed from the fracas, and there was heat in her veins. Sweet reasonableness was forgotten as she faced the woman she disliked.

'You're angry because it was Timmy I stood up for,' she accused.

'If you recognise the problem, then let's hope you're half-way to solving it.'

Virginia's cool tone provoked Alison to an anger she could not control. 'I don't have a problem,' she retorted.

'I disagree. If you've worked with children—as you say you have—then you must know that they have arguments. You'd also know that they should settle them among themselves.'

'Do you really think one little boy can defend himself against five?'

'If he can't, he must learn to. I told you from the start, Alison, that Timmy was to be treated like any other camper.'

'But he's not just any other camper,' Alison countered heatedly. 'He's a little boy who's been through a terrible trauma. He's worried half to death about his parents.'

'Do you think I don't know that? I still say that his best chance for recovery is to be treated normally. Besides'—Virginia paused deliberately—'in a way, what happened was Timmy's own fault. He should have shared his tuck with his friends.'

Alison strove for calm. 'The goodies were from his parents. He didn't want them gobbled up in a minute. He wanted to savour them slowly because they meant so much to him. I'm sure you understand, Virginia.'

'I understand that Timmy means too much to you.'

Which is why you don't like him, Alison realised, but didn't say it.

There was something else she realised. The clash with Virginia only partly concerned Timmy. It concerned Clint, too. And that was something else she could not say to Virginia.

She did not want to admit it even to herself.

CHAPTER SIX

ALISON walked out of Virginia's office, out of the camp grounds.

Taking a seldom-used path up the mountain behind the camp, she walked very quickly, enjoying the wind in her hair and the sting of cool air against her face. She came to a densely wooded area where the wind hardly penetrated, but, by the time she emerged from the trees on to almost barren cliff, the wind was blowing much harder.

'Alison! Alison, wait! Alison...'

She did not know quite when she realised that someone was shouting her name. Pausing, she looked back—and there was Clint.

Clint? The breath stopped quite suddenly in her lungs. She had not even known he was back.

Reaching her, he gripped her shoulders in his hands. His eyes were sparkling and his hair was as windblown as her own. So attractive did he look that Alison's pulses began to beat a crazy tattoo that was becoming rapidly familiar. Deep inside her pleasure burgeoned. It was a pleasure that seemed centred in the very core of her being.

She was unable to keep the sparkle from her own eyes. 'Clint! When did you get back?' she asked.

'Half an hour ago.'

'I didn't know. That must have been just after I left.' She tilted her head back so that she could look at him.

'Good grief, Clint! Did you really say half an hour? Why aren't you at camp, then? What on earth are you doing up here?'

'Looking for you, of course.'

The pleasure deepened. 'Really?'

'Really. Do you always walk so fast when you're upset?'

'How did you know I was upset?'

He grinned. 'Wasn't difficult.'

The sparkle vanished from her eyes. 'Virginia told you. And I'm willing to bet "upset" wasn't the word she used. She probably said I was having one of my tantrums.'

'Something to that effect,' Clint agreed. He turned her around in his hands. 'Look, we can't talk now. In your hurry to walk off your fury, did you never stop to think of taking the weather into account?'

The weather? Why, yes, she'd been aware of the wind, but only in as much as its wildness suited the wildness of her mood. Now, for the first time, she actually took in her surroundings. Clouds, dark and heavy, hung ominously over the high peaks, and in the air was the smell of rain.

'You must know that storms blow up out of nowhere in the mountains, but it seems you were in no mood to notice. Have to make a dash for it, Alison.'

They started back in the direction of the camp, running wherever the path was smooth, walking when they came to low rocks beneath the scrub, Clint in the lead, Alison close behind him. And all the time the air grew colder, while the wind became something of a gale.

'OK?' Clint shouted once, looking over his shoulder at Alison.

'Fine!' she called back.

In fact, his long legs were able to cover more ground than hers, so that her breath was coming in gasps with the effort to keep up with him. But now that she was aware of the storm—had she been out of her mind not to have realised earlier what was coming?—she saw that she had climbed much higher than she had realised. Even if they did not make it all the way back to camp, at least it was important for them to reach lower, less exposed ground before the storm struck.

The first hard raindrops came pelting down when they were still quite some distance from the camp grounds. Lightning sparked alarmingly, and thunder bounced and echoed against the mountains. Alison understood how lucky she was that Clint had found her when he had, while there was still time to leave the high, bare ground where a human being would have been a magnet for lightning. They were back in densely wooded terrain now and, though trees were always potentially lethal in a storm, here they were so thickly clustered that no particular tree would be a target.

Alison was frightened when the hail began; hail could be a killer. She gasped when Clint shoved her roughly to the ground and threw his body over hers.

She did not know how long they lay there. It seemed like an age, though perhaps it was just minutes. With Clint's body shielding her own, she could see nothing. The only reality was the dreadful noise—the booming of the thunder, the creaking of the trees, the lashing of the hail. It was as if all the fury of hell had descended on this one spot.

At last the worst of the storm began to subside. The hail stopped as suddenly as it had begun, and the lightning must have moved to another part of the mountains, for the thunder no longer sounded quite so savage. It was still raining hard, but at least rain wasn't dangerous.

When Clint lifted himself away from her, Alison sat up. Anxiously, she looked at him.

'Are you all right?' she shouted through the roar of the rain.

'Yes.' Incredibly, he was smiling at her. 'Let's find some shelter.'

Her eyes scanned the mountainside. 'The nearest place is the camp.'

Clint was already walking, but to her surprise he was not taking the direct route back to Bushveld. Half a mile on and they came to a ramshackle structure. The shack was set well away from the path, and was hidden by trees, so that Alison realised why she hadn't suspected its existence. She understood too why they hadn't sheltered here through the worst of the storm. To reach the shack would have meant crossing more barren ground, and they might well have been killed on the way.

With a little heaving on Clint's part, the door finally opened. It was a relief to get inside, and away from the punishing rain.

To Alison's amazement, the hut was reasonably clean. There were even a few basic items—an old bed with what looked like a clean grey blanket covering it, a Primus stove, a few cups.

'I've used the place sometimes,' said Clint, seeing her surprise. 'When things have been a bit hectic at Bushveld, and I've felt like a couple of days alone.'

'To shelter from a storm when an impulsive girl walked further than she should have?'

'That, too. Don't you have any nice, docile qualities, Alison?'

'Doesn't seem like it,' she said ruefully.

His eyes sparkled. 'Perhaps that's why I like you so much.'

They looked at each other, and burst out laughing at the same time. And then Alison remembered the hail, and her laughter stopped in her throat. She took a step towards Clint. 'Are you all right?' she asked.

'Yes, of course.'

'I'm not sure I believe that. All that hail—you must have been hurt.'

He touched a hand gingerly to the back of his head. 'Well, maybe a little.'

'God, Clint, this is all my fault!' she exclaimed. 'If it hadn't been for my stupid temper, this wouldn't have happened. I want to look at your back.'

'If you must. But it's not too bad. We were fortunate, Alison, the trees blocked out a lot of the hail.'

'And your body blocked out all of it for me. Let me see your back, Clint.'

He stepped away from the wall, and as he turned Alison drew in her breath. His shirt and trousers were torn. On his back and his legs and even in his hair there was some blood.

'Take off your clothes,' she ordered, as calmly as she was able.

'The very thing I keep wanting to say to you!'

His voice was teasingly seductive, so that Alison thought perhaps he meant it when he said he wasn't badly hurt. Still, she had to be certain.

'Take off your clothes, Clint.'

He began to unbutton his shirt, but when he tried to draw it away from his shoulders he winced.

'I'll do that,' she offered quickly.

'Be my guest,' he invited provocatively. 'Let's see how good you are at undressing me. I've always wanted to know.'

Ignoring the ridiculous way her senses leaped at the words, Alison undressed him gently. Beneath her fingers his skin was warm, and it came to her that she'd touched Clint often in her dreams—those wretched dreams which she was so completely unable to control.

Wordlessly, she surveyed the damage the hail had caused, and tears formed in her throat.

Altogether without thinking, she stepped closer, and pressed her lips against the bare skin between his shoulders.

A shudder shot through the long male body as Clint went suddenly rigid. 'Hey, I think I should get hurt more often,' he said huskily.

'Don't you dare!' Alison was trembling, as shocked as he was at her unexpected action.

'That felt so good. Kiss me again, Alison.'

'It's all the kissing you're going to get from me.'

'Come here...' He had turned, and was reaching for her.

'No!' The blood was pounding hard in her veins, but she managed to keep out of his arms. 'There's some cleaning up to do.'

'Alison, you started something.'

'I didn't mean to. Don't make anything of it.'

Dodging him, she pulled her shirt from the waistband of her jeans, and ripped off a piece of it. Then she went to the door of the shack and held the cloth into the rain.

Very gently, she began to wipe the drying blood from Clint's back. When the cleaning up was done at last, Alison was relieved to find that he had been right, after all—the worst of the hail had been blocked by the trees, and he wasn't as badly hurt as she'd feared.

'That's it,' she said at last.

'Not quite.'

She looked at him. 'Is there something else you want me to do for you?'

'Something very important.' His eyes glinted. 'There's the matter of that kiss.'

His arms went around her, staying around her even when Alison tried to step away from him.

'The kiss didn't mean anything,' she said unsteadily.

'It did to me.'

'I wish you'd forget the kiss, Clint...'

His only answer was in his hands as they began to move over her, slowly, tantalisingly, exploring the sweet curves of her body; curving around her hips and her waist, touching her breasts, but so fleetingly that she did not have time to protest.

The long fingers were leaving a trail of fire on her skin. Alison's nerves had never felt more fragile. She wanted nothing more than to bury her hands in the damp, dark hair on Clint's head, to hold his head against her breast.

Still holding her in the circle of his arms, he sat down on the bed, gathering her on to his lap at the same time. One hand tightened around her back, while with the other he brought her face towards his.

Much as Alison wanted him to kiss her, she knew that she had to resist him. She tried to turn her face away from him, only to gasp when Clint's tongue brushed a sensuous path downwards along her throat, coming to rest in the hollow where her pulse beat with telltale frenzy.

Mindlessly Alison turned to him, wanting to tell him to stop before she lost her sanity. Clint seized his chance. His kiss was hungry, passionate; she could feel his frustration because she did not give him the response he wanted. One hand slid beneath her shirt and, cupping a breast, began to caress a soft nipple to hardness.

Alison's emotions were raw. Her throat was so dry that each breath was agony. Yet some small vestige of sanity remained, and she knew that for her own peace of mind she had to resist him.

Somehow she managed to push a little away from him. 'You have to stop this, Clint.' There was despair in her voice now.

His arms were still around her. 'You're asking the impossible,' he said huskily. 'I want so badly to make love to you. More than ever before.'

'The answer is no—it's always been no. You know how I feel.'

'I was hoping that kiss on my back meant you'd started to change your mind.'

'I'll never change my mind,' she insisted.

'I believe I can make you change it.'

He was bending to kiss her again, but Alison wriggled away from him and stood up. There was a part of her that wanted quite desperately to let Clint make love to her. Which meant that, more than ever, she had to resist him.

'It's no good, Clint. I wish you'd believe me.'

Unfortunately it was still raining. For a while longer they would have to wait in the shack.

She looked around her. 'Don't you keep any supplies in this place?' She had walked away from the bed by now.

Clint's breathing was a little ragged, but he did not try to force her back to him. 'A few. There's the Primus stove, instant coffee, a couple of mugs.'

'Wonderful! Let's have some coffee.' Her voice was determinedly bright.

'Still running away from me,' he observed wryly. 'Are you really so scared of me, Alison?'

Scared? The word was an understatement. She was absolutely terrified of the things he could make her feel! It was growing harder and harder to stop herself falling in love with him.

Somehow she managed a little laugh. 'Scared? Of course I'm not scared. Look, Clint, I don't know about you, but I'm cold. Shall we get some coffee started?'

Without a word, Clint hauled out the old Primus stove, which he kept clean and filled. While he lit it, Alison held a saucepan into the rain. When the water was boiling, she made the coffee.

Clint sat down on the bed once more. Other than the floor, which was thick with dust, there was nowhere to sit, but Alison had no intention of being so close to him again. So she remained standing near the warm Primus and, while they drank their coffee, she steered the conversation to safe subjects.

She told Clint about the overnight trail-ride she was in the process of organising, and then Clint told her a little about his trip. They spent some minutes talking about Timmy, and he was glad to hear how well the little boy was adjusting to camp life.

After a while, Alison turned the subject to the incident of the afternoon. 'Before the storm...you were going to tell me what Virginia said. I suppose she told you what happened?'

'She did.'

'I don't think I was wrong to defend Timmy, Clint.'

'You weren't,' he assured her.

'I don't suppose you said that to Virginia.'

'No, I didn't.' The look he gave her was steady. 'And you know the reason for that. I know Virginia ran the camp well in my absence, and she'll keep running it for me.'

'You rely on Virginia, yet sometimes I wonder...is that the only reason you keep defending her?'

'Come on, Alison!'

But something drove her to continue. 'Why did you come looking for me when you'd just got back to camp, Clint? To give me a lecture about Virginia?'

'I came because I couldn't get you off my mind all the time I was away,' he said, very softly.

'You expect me to believe that?' But the hard words belied her pleasure.

'Of course. After my lovemaking, I wouldn't have thought you'd need to ask.'

Alison was beginning to tremble. 'Lovemaking is just something men enjoy doing. It doesn't necessarily mean anything.'

He was watching her, his eyes hard to read. 'Still the same Alison,' he commented.

'You didn't think I'd change, did you?'

'I was hoping you had.'

Abruptly, Alison stood up and went to the door of the shack. Mountain storms began and ended very quickly, and she saw that the rain had almost stopped. All that was left was a weak drizzle.

She was about to tell Clint that they could go back to camp, when he came up behind her. She did not turn when he gripped her shoulders.

'Why don't you believe me when I say I couldn't get you off my mind?' His lips moved in her hair.

'I don't know what to believe.' Her voice was choked.

'I'll have to prove it to you, then.'

'By trying to kiss me again?' she asked tensely.

'By showing you something I've never shown anyone else.'

She turned. 'What?'

The corners of his lips lifted in the smile that had become so familiar, she had seen it in her dreams every night while he was away. 'Are you up to a climb?'

Her curiosity was aroused. 'If you are. What about your back?'

Clint laughed softly. 'That kiss did wonders for my back! Come on, let's go.'

Alison was even more curious when they left the shack and began to walk, not towards the camp, but in the direction of a distant gorge. This was one way she had never been before.

There was no trail, not even the faintest sign of a path, yet Clint seemed to know exactly where he was going. Underfoot the wild grass was wet from the rain, and the air was spicy with the scent of mountain shrubs. Here and there, water cascaded down cliffsides that would have been barren save for the aloes and cacti that grew between the rocks.

Alison stopped now and then to look around her at a scene that was wilder and more desolate than anything she had yet encountered. It was as if no human feet had ever trod this ground.

'Why won't you tell me where we're going?'

Clint's grin was wicked. 'Because that would ruin the surprise.'

At a high cleft at the very end of the narrow gorge, he turned and reached a hand to her.

'This is it?' she asked incredulously.

'It's as far as we go. Come on up.'

Alison let him help her up the rock-face. He was still holding her hand when she peered through the cleft. Far below them was nothing but a windswept plateau.

Mystified, she looked at Clint. His eyes sparkled back at her. 'Not long to wait.'

'Wait for *what*?'

'You'll see.'

'The suspense is killing me, Clint!' she laughed.

'Really?' He threw her the most maddening grin as he pointed to a rocky ledge. 'Might as well make ourselves comfortable in the meantime. Let's sit down.'

They had to sit very close together on the small piece of rock wedged between two high cliffs. Alison was beginning to wonder how long they would have to wait, when a noise sounded from the plateau far below.

A rumbling sound, a little like thunder, faint at first, getting louder by the second.

Hooves! Within moments a string of horses hurtled into sight. Eight, perhaps ten.

Horses unlike any Alison had ever seen—wild horses, horses which did not answer to commands, which had never known saddles or bridles. Untamed, free, heads thrust high, tails streaming behind them, galloping like the mountain wind across the desolate plateau.

As quickly as they had come, they vanished. In less than a minute they were out of sight.

Alison expelled a breath she hadn't known she was holding, as she turned a wordless look to Clint.

'Wild horses,' he confirmed.

'They're incredible! Absolutely incredible! How did they get here?'

'I can't tell you for certain. My guess is that years ago they must have escaped from a ranch. Perhaps someone stole them, and then had to let them loose for some reason. I don't know.'

'And no effort was ever made to recapture them?'

'If there was, I don't know about it.'

'What a sight! Clint, did you mean it when you said you'd never brought anyone else up here?'

'Yes, I meant it.'

'Why not?' she asked.

'Because there's never been anybody I wanted to share the horses with.'

Alison's throat was thick with a sudden rush of emotion. Unsteadily, she said, 'Thank you.'

'Was it worth the climb, Alison?' Clint's voice was soft.

'Absolutely!' Her eyes shone. 'I've never seen anything so beautiful.'

'As you are the most beautiful girl I've ever seen,' he said huskily.

'Don't...' she began.

'You're so like the horses, Alison.'

Her heartbeats quickened. 'In what way?'

'Beautiful, independent, wild and free.'

She drew a shuddering breath. 'You're talking nonsense.'

'Yet shy, too. The horses didn't see us. They'd take fright if they did. Just as as you take fright whenever you're with me.'

'This really is nonsense, Clint.'

Narrow as the ledge was, he managed to put his arm around her shoulder. 'I really did miss you all the time I was away. Did you miss me at all, Alison?'

Her heart was beating so hard that it felt as if it would burst right out of her chest. 'No,' she said. And then, 'Well, maybe a little.'

His lips nuzzled her hair. 'That's something. The first time you've actually let yourself acknowledge some feeling!'

'Don't make too much of it,' she said quickly.

'You'd pull me up fast enough if I did, wouldn't you? But I *am* going to kiss you, Alison, and unless you want to risk falling off this ledge, you won't be able to stop me.'

But, as Clint began to kiss her, it was the intensity of her emotions, rather than the precariousness of the ledge, which stopped Alison from pulling away from him.

Clint's free hand cupped her face as his lips began to explore hers, seemingly gently at first, yet so tantalisingly that the blood turned to maddened fire in her veins. There was little room to move, wedged in as they were between the cliffs, yet Clint did not let that hinder him.

Gentleness turned quickly to passion. The kisses became harder, more urgent. His tongue pushed at her lips, seeking entrance to the sweetness of her mouth. He was taking her—still quivering with emotion from their encounter in the shack—to heights where resistance was becoming impossible. With the blood drumming in her head, Alison finally opened her lips to him.

A harsh, hissing breath tore his throat, and he lifted his head and looked down at her. 'You're so beautiful,' he groaned huskily. 'The most beautiful woman in the world.'

Eyes smudged with shock, she looked at him wordlessly, and then away. She did not want him to see the emotions he had aroused in her, for if he did she'd be left with no more defences.

His head came down, and he was kissing her again, demanding the response which she was no longer able to deny him. A primeval hunger throbbed within her. She *wanted* Clint to kiss her, there was a part of her that wished he would never stop.

At length, he lifted his head. 'You're driving me insane,' he muttered.

'I'm not feeling exactly lucid myself right now,' she managed.

'Kissing's fine, Alison, but I want so much more from you.'

'On this ledge?' She attempted an amused laugh, but it didn't quite come off.

'We could go back to the shack.'

'No, Clint.'

'It's what we both want,' he insisted huskily.

'It's what *you* want,' she corrected.

'You do too, Alison. You were responding to me.'

She looked at him a little wildly. 'Clint, I wish...I wish you'd forget everything that happened today.'

'Do you think you can forget it?' he demanded.

She wouldn't forget it till the day she died.

'I hope so,' she shrugged.

'I don't believe you will. I know Raymond hurt you badly, but to shut yourself away from life because of him is wrong.'

She lifted troubled eyes. 'I've gone further today than I ever thought I would. But don't force me into anything, Clint—please! I couldn't bear it.'

He was silent a few moments before saying, 'I promised you once I wouldn't do that. Remember?'

'Yes...'

'Which doesn't mean I won't keep hoping.' He touched her arm. 'Come along, Alison, let's get back to camp.'

Later that evening, Virginia detained Alison as she was walking to her cabin. 'I've been looking for you, Alison. How are you getting on with your plans for the overnight ride?'

'Very well.' It seemed like an odd time to discuss the ride.

'I'd like to see a list of the supplies you intend taking with you.'

'I've made it up. I'll give it to you,' Alison said politely.

'Also the names of all those who will be going,' added Virginia.

'Yes, all right. I'll have the lists in your office first thing in the morning, Virginia.'

Alison was on the point of walking on, when Virginia stopped her. 'You were away from camp a long time this afternoon.'

Alison maintained her politeness. 'I'd given all my lessons for the day.'

'Clint was gone, too. He came back from his trip, then took off again in a hurry.' Uncharacteristically, Virginia hesitated a moment. 'Were you together?'

So this was why the other girl had waylaid her! Alison decided to remain silent.

Virginia gave a harsh laugh. 'You have in fact just answered the question. There's something you should know, Alison. Clint isn't a one-woman man.'

Alison looked at her with distaste. 'I don't know why you're telling me this. It doesn't concern me one way or another.'

'I think you should know—he was married once.'

'I do know.'

Virginia looked surprised. 'He told you?'

'Yes, he did.'

'Then you understand that if he'd wanted to marry again, he'd have done so years ago?'

Alison was finding it increasingly hard to retain her composure. 'I really don't know what you're getting at, Virginia. None of this has anything to do with me.'

'I don't believe that. You're the kind of girl who wants marriage.' Virginia's husky voice was hard. 'Marriage, babies, a settled home, a faithful and adoring husband to support you. You have commitment written all over your face.'

'Actually, I take pride in being independent,' Alison said coldly. 'What's the purpose of all this, Virginia?'

'I don't want to see you get hurt. Clint is human, he likes attractive women—but it never goes further than that, take my word for it. Even if the two of you are— friends—it won't last longer than the end of camp.'

'That's fine with me,' said Alison, as calmly as she could. 'The fact is, I'm not looking for a husband, I have my own plans for the future, and I have absolutely no interest in commitment.'

'Then you're not in love with him?'

The happiness that had been with Alison all afternoon was gone now. She lifted her chin. 'All these questions, just because we happened to spend an afternoon together? I really don't think it's any of your concern, Virginia, but no, I am not in love with Clint.'

CHAPTER SEVEN

THE SUN was just rising when the trail-riders left camp. Alison rode at the head of the group, the reins of a pack-horse held in one hand. Behind her were fifteen of the older campers. It was the start of the overnight trail-ride which this group had been looking forward to since the beginning of camp. Tonight they would be sleeping on a high mountain slope beneath the stars.

The mist was just lifting from the high peaks when Alison called a breakfast halt at one of the many rest stops Clint had created along the way—this was one route where people would never find themselves stranded without shelter in the event of an unexpected storm!

After tethering both her own horse and the pack-horse to a post, Alison went to help the two senior boys, Fraser and Alex, who had been given the responsibility of leading the two other pack-horses.

'Did you know a brown snake eagle has been sighted around here, Alison? Boy, what I wouldn't give to see it!' Fraser bubbled with anticipation.

Alison smiled at him. Sixteen years old, and a regular Bushveld camper since he'd been old enough to leave home, Fraser had quickly endeared himself to her. He loved horses, but his real passion was birds. He spent his free time tramping the veld around the camp, binoculars to his eyes, a camera slung around his neck. Alison, who liked birds too, knew that the brown snake eagle was the one bird Fraser had been longing to see since the beginning of camp.

'Maybe you'll be lucky,' she told him, as she took a thermos and a stack of plastic glasses from one of the saddle-bags. 'Just have to keep watching.'

The campers crowded around her excitedly, chattering, laughing, eager for hot cocoa and sandwiches. Alison smiled as she listened to them. So intensely had they been looking forward to this overnight trip that each one had been dressed and ready long before dawn.

The thought of the two days away from Bushveld pleased Alison as much as it did her group—though the reason differed. Since the afternoon when he had taken her to see the wild horses, she was finding it harder and harder to get Clint out of her mind. It was no longer possible to deny to herself that she was physically attracted to him. But physical attraction was all it was, she kept telling herself. She *did not love* Clint. She had no intention of falling in love with him. Still, with her strength of will so fragile these days, she was glad of the chance to be away from him for two days.

It was midday when they reached the resting stop where they would spend the night. After unloading the pack-horses and storing the supplies, they would pitch the tents, then they would spend the remainder of the afternoon exploring on horseback, before returning to the rest stop for the evening *braaivleis* and camp-fire.

Alison was tethering her pack-horse when she heard Fraser's ecstatic cry.

'A brown snake eagle—wow! Look!'

'Where?' came other cries.

'Up there—on the cliff. It's actually holding a snake in its talons. Oh, wow!'

Alison turned her head. But she never saw the eagle, as her horrified eyes fastened on the pack-horse Fraser had been leading. In his excitement, the boy's hand had loosened on the rein, and the horse had broken away from him.

'Fraser—the horse!' she shouted.

But it was too late. Even as the startled boy turned and tried to make a grab, the pack-horse was heading full speed down the mountain slope in the direction of the camp.

'Oh, Lord!' he groaned. 'That horse has all our precious water! I'll have to go after it.'

Alison stopped him as he was about to get back on his own horse. 'No, Fraser, I'll go.'

'But it was my fault. I saw the eagle, and I...I suppose I got distracted. I just forgot I was holding the reins. Let me try and catch the horse, Alison.'

She put her hand on his arm. 'You're my responsibility, Fraser. I can't have you riding through the mountains alone.'

'At least let me come with you,' he insisted.

'No, you're the oldest here, and the most responsible. I want you and Alex to look after the others. Get the horses tethered, and then perhaps you could start a game of some kind going. Nobody is to get back on a horse till I return—that's an order.'

'Some kind of responsible I am!' Fraser was crestfallen.

Alison touched his cheek gently. 'Hey, it's not every day a person sees a brown snake eagle. You're forgiven, Fraser, so don't be too hard on yourself. Look, I can't stay here talking. I have to get after that darn horse, maybe I can catch up with it before it gets to camp.'

But the pack-horse arrived at the stables before Alison did. Waiting for her, looking anxious, were Clint and Virginia.

'What *happened*?' Virginia demanded.

'The horse decided it preferred to be here rather than on the mountain. Unfortunately, all our water went with it.'

'It shouldn't have happened,' Virginia accused. 'Why weren't you more careful?'

Before Alison could answer, Clint asked, 'Are *you* all right, Alison?'

She smiled up at him. 'Exasperated, but otherwise OK.'

'I'm more concerned about my campers.' Virginia looked grim. 'Where are they? How do I know they're all right?'

'They're all at rest stop number four. I've left Fraser and Alex in charge, with instructions that nobody is to ride until I get back.'

'Which must be immediately.'

'I intend leaving right away, Virginia,' Alison said evenly.

'I'll ride along with you,' Clint announced unexpectedly.

'That isn't necessary,' protested Alison.

'I don't want you riding back alone.'

'You shouldn't have to go, Clint,' Virginia said quickly, her tone oddly high. 'If Alison had taken proper care, this wouldn't have happened.'

'I think we both know Alison had nothing to do with it,' Clint said easily. 'She's far too competent to let a horse get away from her. Who was the culprit, Alison— Fraser or Alex?'

Alison shot a glance at Virginia, then bit her lip. 'I was leading the group.'

'That's correct,' said Virginia. 'I don't like to think of those kids on the mountain alone. I really wish you'd get going, Alison.'

'In a moment.' There was authority in Clint's tone. 'Give me a few moments to saddle up first.'

'It really isn't necessary,' Alison said again.

'As far as I'm concerned, it is. I don't like the thought of you riding all that way alone. Wait for me—I'll just be a minute.'

Virginia's colour was high, the look she shot Alison angry, as Clint walked purposefully into the stables. She opened her mouth, then closed it again tightly, and strode away.

'How did you know what happened wasn't my fault?' Alison asked.

The man riding beside her, holding the rein of the pack-horse in one hand, turned his head and flashed a grin that made her heart turn over. 'I know *you*,' he told her.

'I appreciate your confidence.'

'So formal, Alison?' He chuckled. 'You never did say—was it Fraser or Alex?'

'Fraser. I couldn't tell Virginia.' She told him about the eagle. 'You're not going to be angry with Fraser, are you?'

Clint was still laughing at the story. 'Why would I be angry? Heavens, no! I can see exactly how it happened.' Leaning towards her, he touched her hand briefly. 'Besides, I'm grateful to young Fraser. I think you know how glad I am to be riding with you.'

It didn't seem to matter that Alison had wanted two days away from him. Happiness filled her heart, spreading like a warm, living thing through her entire body. The air was more sparkling all at once, the sky more vividly blue. Alison had to look away from Clint because she didn't want him to see that her eyes were shining.

It was quite late in the afternoon when they reached the fourth rest stop, and Alison was relieved to see that everything had gone smoothly in her absence.

She had imagined Clint would return to camp as soon as he had satisfied himself that all was well with the children, but to her surprise he showed no sign of leaving. He let Fraser lead him a little way up a bare cliffside, for a good view of the eagle. And after that he told the campers to get on their horses, and, with Alison riding beside him, led them all along a beautiful trail.

The first gold wash of sunset stained the sky by the time they got back to the rest stop. And still Clint showed no sign of leaving.

'You're not giving yourself much time to get back to camp before dark,' Alison worried.

He grinned. 'You sound like a wife!'

'Which I'm not,' she said, a little crossly.

'I didn't say I object.'

A sudden trembling went through her body, but she brought it quickly under control. A little too matter-of-factly she said, 'I just happen to be concerned.'

He tugged lightly at a strand of hair which had fallen across her forehead. 'Don't be. I know how to take care of myself.'

Half an hour later he was still there. By now the sky was a brilliant palette of colour. The highest peaks were bathed in golden light, but the lower slopes looked grey and cold.

Alison was really anxious now. 'You can't leave it any longer, Clint. If you do, you'll have to stay the night.'

'Would you mind?'

'Mind? Why should I mind? But you didn't bring anything with you.'

'No pyjamas,' he teased. 'No toothpaste. Not even a toothbrush.'

'You're laughing at me. But you know quite well what I mean—you don't have a sleeping-bag. You could freeze up here on the mountain, Clint.'

'I could cuddle up with you.' His tone was teasingly seductive.

Her blood raced at the picture his words conjured. 'Even if I'd let you do that—which I wouldn't—there are all the children to consider.'

He burst out laughing. 'What a bundle of contradictions you are, Alison! Nonconforming and free like the wild horses one moment, concerned about social norms the next.'

'You *are* laughing at me.'

'I'm crazy about you, don't you know?'

She decided to ignore that. 'What *are* you going to do without a sleeping-bag, Clint?'

He laughed again. 'Coward! Every time I fire a personal question at you, you find a way of evading it. As for freezing—I'll find a way of surviving, Alison. It won't be the first night I've spent in the open.'

The sunset faded and with darkness it grew cold. A few of the campers brought out logs and coal from the rest stop, and Clint helped them make a fire in a special pit. Others were delegated to look after the horses and see that they were watered and fed.

When the flames were low and the burning coal had turned to grey, Alison brought out the food. Steak and chops sizzled and spat on the hot grid of the pit, and *mielies*, parboiled the day before, were put out to be reheated.

When they had all finished eating, Clint threw more logs on the fire and let the flames burn high once more. Shouts of glee greeted a bag of marshmallows produced by Alison, and while the the campers sat round the fire roasting them, Clint started a sing-song.

But the long hours in the saddle had taken their toll. One after another, the campers took their sleeping bags and retired to their tents; girls in one tent, boys in another. Alison waited a while, then went into each tent in turn. Everyone was sleeping soundly.

Going back to the fire, she sat down beside Clint. He put his arm around her and drew her head against his shoulder, and she didn't resist him. She could easily have spent the night snuggled against him, so good did it feel to be close to him.

It required all her effort to say eventually, 'I think I'll turn in, too.'

His hand tightened on her shoulder, bringing her round to face him. His kiss was so seductively sweet that she had to restrain herself from putting her arms around his neck and asking for more.

Somehow she managed to lift her head from his shoulder. 'This isn't a good idea, Clint,' she said quietly.

'Because of the kids? They're all in their tents and asleep. There's not a soul watching us.'

'Yes, but still, I don't think we should...'

His next kiss was a heady onslaught, silencing her words and pouring fire through her loins. His arm tightened around her, turning her into his body. His free hand touched her throat, the fingers trailing a sensuous path along the most sensitive part of it. And then his lips traced the same path. He seemed to know all the most sensitive areas—the arch of her throat, the little hollow where her pulse beat a crazy rhythm, her eyelids and the soft skin behind her ears.

Alison was trembling as she began to touch him in turn. There was a quite intense pleasure in the feel of his cool skin beneath her fingers, the hardness of bone and muscle in his chest and shoulders. She could feel his beating heart against her chest, and her own heart seemed to pound in unison with it.

He was still kissing her, kisses that shook her to the depths of her being with their sensuousness. Kisses that were drawing a response from her—for the first time she was kissing him back without reserve. She would never have believed that any man could make her feel so abandoned that nothing mattered except the pleasure they could give each other. But Clint was doing just that.

'God, this is frustrating!' he groaned suddenly. 'I want so much more than this. If only there weren't the kids to consider! We should have been alone up here.'

The words brought back some semblance of sanity. 'I wish you weren't here at all. I wish you hadn't come with me, Clint,' Alison said softly.

'Because you want something that you won't allow yourself to enjoy?'

'Something like that . . .' she admitted shakily.

'You were responding just now.'

'I . . . I couldn't seem to help it.' Her lips quivered.

'Let's give it another try,' he coaxed softly.

She made herself move away from him, and wished it wasn't such an effort. 'I'll be sorry afterwards if I do.'

'Do you realise that it's not me you're fighting, Alison?' he asked huskily. 'You're fighting yourself every time. And the memory of a man who behaved very badly.'

She stood up abruptly. 'I'm going to my tent.'

'When will you stop fighting yourself? When will you see that it's a losing battle?'

Through lips that still quivered, she managed to say, 'The battle's not lost yet. Goodnight, Clint.'

'Sleep well, Alison,' he returned softly, as she went to her own tiny tent.

She did not sleep at all. Fitfully she tossed and turned in the snug comfort of her down sleeping-bag, and twice she peeped through the opening of the tent and looked across at Clint. He lay on a spare groundsheet beside the dying fire, covered only by his windbreaker and the jacket Alison had insisted on giving him. She had no way of knowing whether he was asleep.

Finally she could stand it no longer. Cursing herself for being a fool, she got up and went to him.

Touching his arm, she whispered, 'Come and share my sleeping-bag with me.'

Beneath her fingers, she felt a muscle go rigid. 'Will you regret this later?' he asked.

'Probably. But I mightn't be able to live with myself if you froze to death out here in the cold.'

Clint's laugh was soft and amused. 'I never thought it would be conscience that would get me into your bed!'

They unzipped Alison's bag and spread it flat on the groundsheet, then they lay down, side by side, underneath it.

Alison lay quite still, achingly aware of the long male body so close to her. Deep inside her, a primeval longing grew stronger all the time. It was a longing that seemed centred in the very core of her being.

'I suppose you expected I'd come for you, Clint?' she asked him quietly.

'I hoped you would,' he admitted.

'We can't let the children wake in the morning and find us together like this.'

'I'll make quite sure that I leave you long before they wake up,' he promised. 'Not a soul will ever know that we spent the night together.'

They spoke softly, so that the campers asleep in their tents would not hear them.

'Just one thing, Clint... Don't think that because I let you... What I mean is...don't start anything.'

'I won't overstep the limits,' he promised. 'I know there are fifteen impressionable youngsters nearby.'

Alison shifted restlessly on the groundsheet. 'I was just making certain.'

'Which is not to say I wouldn't like to do more.'

His thumb went to her throat, stroking along it so tantalisingly that Alison's blood turned to liquid fire in her veins.

'And some day we will,' he added. 'And don't tell me that's unlikely!'

Filling her nostrils was an exciting smell that said Clint. It dizzied her senses, inflaming emotions that were already raw.

'Do you know how desirable you are?' His hand was stroking lower now, sliding beneath the collar of her sweater. 'It's going to be sheer hell, lying beside you all night and unable to do anything about it.'

It would be hell for her too, but she had no intention of letting him know it.

She jerked convulsively when he pushed the shirt from her jeans—for she had not changed her clothes—and caressed the smooth, bare skin of her stomach. Then he folded his arm around her, letting his hand rest on her breast. She began to tremble.

'Clint, you promised!' Her voice was choked.

'I won't do more than this,' he whispered against her ear.

'Even this is too much.'

'No, darling, it's just a beginning. But we'll come up here again some time, just you and I. And maybe then you'll be ready to let me show you how I feel about you.'

Alison did not answer, and she was relieved when he did not comment on her silence. The tumultuous demands of her body had brought her to a point where she did not know how much longer she could go on resisting him.

'I want to sleep,' she whispered tensely.

'Goodnight.'

She wondered if Clint would move away from her, but his arm stayed where it was, holding her. After a while his breathing grew slow and regular, and she was sure he must be asleep.

Alison turned on to her side. She was shaken when the long body turned with hers, Clint's arm tightening its hold against her breast, his chest hard against her back, his legs curling beneath hers.

Every nerve was throbbing inside her now, she was so totally conscious of him—the whipcord male strength encircling her body, the sound of his breathing in her ear, the warmth of every breath he took on the back of her neck. They could have been one body folded together beneath her sleeping-bag.

Amazingly, she did fall asleep at last. When she woke up it was very early morning, and she was alone beneath the sleeping-bag. Clint had been true to his word. He had got up and left her long before dawn, so that none of the campers would ever know that they had shared the same tent.

Minutes later he appeared in the tent. 'Coffee?' He was squatting beside her, holding out a steaming mug.

Sitting up, she took it from him gratefully. 'You have a beard starting,' she laughed.

He bent towards her and rubbed his cheek against hers, the unshaven stubble excitingly rough against her smooth skin.

'A preview of what it would be like to wake up beside me after a night of love,' he grinned.

'Since that's not going to happen, the preview wasn't necessary.'

But the fact was that the treacherous thought had indeed crossed her mind.

When they'd finished their coffee and rolled up Alison's sleeping-bag, it was time to start waking the campers. Clint had made a new fire, and the youngsters crowded round it, warming their hands and drinking hot cocoa while Alison scrambled up a huge batch of eggs.

They spent the morning on the mountain, but by midday it was time to start the ride back to camp.

'Can't we spend one more night on the mountain?' begged the youngsters.

But Alison resisted all their pleas. Even when Clint's laughing eyes caught hers, she remained firm in her refusal. One night in the company of this man whom she would never see again after camp ended had been devastating. Another night could well destroy her altogether!

CHAPTER EIGHT

'LET'S go up to the hotel for a while.' It was Brian who made the suggestion.

The rest of the counsellors were enthusiastic. 'Clint won't mind if we take the jeep,' said Gary.

The evening camp-fire had burned itself out by then. Only the night-watchman was needed in the grounds at this hour, for the younger children were in bed, and the older campers, who didn't need active supervision, were in their cabins.

'Coming, Alison?' asked Mary.

'Yes, I'd like to.' She had not seen Clint around—which did not stop her thinking about him—so the diversion was welcome.

Alison was laughing at something Mary said when they walked into the hotel—laughter that stopped in her throat as she looked across the lounge. The big room was crowded, but Alison's eyes took in only two people: Clint and Virginia sitting side by side in a corner, heads inclined in what looked like intense conversation.

Something died inside her at the sight. She felt the blood drain from her cheeks and her legs went weak. Clint chose that very moment to look up—almost as if he'd felt she was watching him. For what seemed like an age, his eyes held hers across the crowded room, and then he was on his feet, and waving them all over.

If it had been up to Alison, she would have ignored the invitation, but the others were already moving across the room towards Clint and Virginia, and she had little option but to follow them.

'Come and join us. Pull up one more chair, Brian, then we should have enough,' Clint was saying.

'I really think we should sit somewhere else,' Alison protested through dry lips.

'Nonsense! It's nice for us all to spend a little time together away from the camp. I was going to suggest we do that one evening, anyway.'

'But not tonight... We... we're intruding.'

'You're not intruding,' Clint said easily. 'Virginia and I came here to talk over some camp affairs, and we'd just finished. Hadn't we, Virginia?' He looked at the camp director for confirmation.

Stunningly beautiful in a flame-red dress that looked as if it had been moulded to her exotic figure, Virginia waited just a moment before saying, 'Yes, of course.'

'I still think we should sit elsewhere,' Alison said unhappily, but by this time Brian had brought the extra chair, and since everyone else was sitting it would have looked odd if she hadn't sat down, too.

'This one's on me,' Clint told them. 'How about a dessert and a liqueur for everyone? What will you all have?'

A few minutes were spent in consulting the menu. The waiter arrived, and the counsellors gave their orders. Alison's appetite had vanished—she asked only for coffee.

'That can't be all you're having, Alison?'

She looked up to find Clint watching her, his eyes thoughtful.

Politely she said, 'Yes, that's all, thank you.'

'Are you sure?'

'Quite sure.'

'Virginia?' Clint asked then.

The camp director smiled at him. 'Oh, the usual for me, Clint.'

He smiled back at her. 'Crème de menthe and cheesecake?'

'Of course.'

The exchange was evocative, the few words and the smiles hinting at an intimacy that could only have developed through a great deal of time spent together. Evenings shared in the past—perhaps even in the present.

Though Alison had always been aware that Clint and Virginia were friends, she was totally unprepared for the attack of jealousy that struck her with all the force of a physical blow. A choking wave of nausea rose in her throat, so that she knew she had to get to the ladies' room. Muttering a plea to be excused, she got quickly to her feet.

Clint caught up with her in a deserted foyer. 'Alison, what's wrong?' he demanded.

She looked at him through pain-filled eyes. 'Nothing— I'm fine.'

'You don't look it.'

'I . . .' Wildly, she cast around for an excuse. 'It's been a long day. I'm just a little tired.'

'You went white all of a sudden.'

'I'm fine, really I am,' she insisted.

'You don't look it,' he said again.

His hands went to her shoulders, holding them. She grew quite rigid for a second, then she stepped backwards quickly, away from him.

His grip tightened. 'Something *is* wrong. We've come a long way since just a touch from me got you all uptight.'

'Nothing's wrong,' Alison assured him.

'Does this have anything to do with the fact that I'm here with Virginia?' His eyes narrowed. 'We're not out on a date together, Alison. We really did come here to talk about camp matters.'

'Maybe so. It really doesn't concern me.'

'Then why are you so upset?'

'I'm not upset.' She tried to say it brightly. She had a sense that she should leave it at that, but some inner demon drove her on. 'Of course, it's obvious there have been dates, though. I mean, you know Virginia's favourite foods. I get the feeling you know each other pretty well.'

His expression was hard to read. 'We've known each other a long time, Alison.'

'And that's the real reason you come to her defence every time, isn't it? I always thought there had to be more to it than just the fact that she's the camp director.'

'If you're asking whether I like Virginia,' Clint said slowly, 'the answer is yes, I do. I like and respect her. But that's not the only reason I defend her. She does have a position of authority at Bushveld, Alison—and I can't let that be undermined. I thought you understood that by now.'

She understood only that Clint and Virginia were good friends. Very good friends indeed.

'Alison, you wouldn't be jealous of Virginia, would you?' There was a new note in Clint's tone.

'*Jealous?*' Alison gave a harsh laugh. 'You can only be jealous if you're in love with someone, and you know how I feel about *that*!'

A muscle tightened in Clint's jaw. 'If it's not Virginia, are you going to tell me why you're upset?'

'I'm not upset,' she lied. 'I told you—I'm tired. I was silly to come tonight in the circumstances. Look, this conversation is really ridiculous. I want to go to the ladies' room. As for you...Virginia, and the others...they must be wondering where you are.'

'I'm going back to them now.'

In the seclusion of the ladies' room, Alison turned on the tap and splashed cold water over her face. Straightening, she took a few deep gulps of breath. At length she leaned back against a wall and covered her eyes with her hands.

The unthinkable had happened. *She had fallen in love with Clint.* And it had taken her jealousy of Virginia to make her admit it to herself.

What she had told herself was just physical attraction had been love all the time. She wondered now how she could have been quite so blind—or so *stupid* as to let herself fall in love with a man whom she would never see again once camp ended.

She was still leaning against the wall when the door opened and Mary came in.

'Alison, are you all right?' she asked anxiously.

Alison dropped her hands from her face. 'Clint asked me the same thing a few minutes ago,' she confessed.

'I couldn't help wondering. You didn't look yourself when you left the table.'

Alison forced a smile. 'It's sweet of you to be concerned, but I'm fine, really I am.'

'Well, all right, then.' If Mary guessed the truth—and
Alison thought it quite probable that she did—she obviously decided not to press the point. 'Shall we go and
join the others?'

Alison caught Clint's questioning look as she sat down.
She answered it with a smile and a light shrug. Not for
the world would she let him know what she had just
found out about herself. She forced herself to laugh and
talk with the others; she even managed to be friendly to
Virginia.

The evening seemed to drag on for ever, but eventually it came to an end. Clint and Virginia left in the
Porsche, while Alison piled into the jeep with the other
counsellors.

They were almost back at Bushveld when Brian said,
'It's my birthday tomorrow. Let's get together tomorrow
night in my cabin when everyone's asleep and have a
party.'

'All the staff?' asked Gary.

'Just the counsellors. Tonight was fun—it was decent
of Clint to pay for us. But I don't think a cabin party
is quite his scene, nor Virginia's. Will you all come?'

Except for Alison, all the counsellors were enthusiastic. 'Thanks for the invitation, but I think you'll have
to count me out,' she said.

'Come on, Alison, we'll have fun!'

Her throat was tight with unshed tears and her head
was throbbing. Fun was the last thing she wanted.
'Thanks,' she said gently, 'but I don't think so.'

Alison slept very little that night, and when she did, her
dreams were all of Clint—dreams that she tried very hard
to forget when she woke up the next morning.

She was on her way to the stables to give a lesson when she ran into him.

'I was looking for you,' he said. 'Feeling better this morning?'

His hair was damp, as if he'd just been for a swim, and he was looking so attractive that Alison had to steel herself very hard to remain unaffected. He was smiling down at her, with that smile that made her want to go into his arms every time she saw it.

She made sure that her answering smile gave nothing away. 'I was just very tired last night.'

'As long as you're not tired tonight.'

She tensed at the words. 'What are you talking about?' she asked.

'I'm hoping for a clear sky tonight. If there is, we'll go up the mountain, just you and I.'

Alison shook her head. 'I don't think so...'

'I told you we'd go up again—remember, Alison? We won't go as far as we went with the kids, of course. But at least we'll be alone this time.'

Hunger began to burn inside her, a savage, aching hunger. She drew a shuddering breath. 'That may not be a very good idea,' she said. 'Imagine what people will say!'

'Why should anyone have anything to say? It's really nobody's business. But if it makes you feel better, I won't come to your cabin to fetch you until everyone is asleep.'

Clint touched her lips with his fingers, then let his hand rest on her throat a moment, very lightly. So erotic was that featherlight touch that the hunger inside her became almost unbearable. She tried very hard to keep her face expressionless, praying that he would not see in her eyes how deeply she longed for him.

'If it clouds over and we can't go up the mountain, we'll just stay in your cabin,' he told her.

'But, Clint . . .'

'No buts, little one. Look, your first pupils are arriving. I'll see you later.'

It was very hard for Alison to keep her mind on the lessons she was giving that morning. She knew only what would happen that night. Clint would try once again to make love to her. And this time, loving him as she did—and despite the fact that there could be only heartbreak for her afterwards—she might not be able to resist him.

She could not let it happen.

The moment her duties for the morning were over, she went in search of Brian.

'Is it all right if I change my mind about joining the party tonight?' she asked him.

He was taken aback, but pleased. 'You mean you'll come?'

'If the invitation is still open.'

'Of course it's open, Alison.'

Alison looked at her watch. It was important that she leave her cabin before Clint arrived.

She was the first to arrive at Brian's cabin, but within minutes the others came, too. The girls had brought popcorn and pretzels and potato chips, and Brian and Gary had laid in a stock of soft drinks and beer. Alison's contribution was a box of chocolates.

In no time the party was under way. Mary had brought her guitar, and she strummed softly while they ate, pausing now and then to eat herself.

After a while, Brian and Gary began to tell naughty stories. Alison did not think they were particularly

amusing, yet she laughed harder than anyone else—
almost as if by doing so she could convince herself that
all was well.

She had gone to pour herself a ginger ale when Mary
came up behind her. 'You're not enjoying this,' she observed very quietly.

Alison pretended surprise. 'I'm having a good time.'

'Did you tell Clint you were coming?'

'Heavens, no!'

Mary—perceptive Mary, who had become her friend—
gave her a steady look. She looked as if she was about
to say more, but Brian came up to them at that moment.

He put an arm around Alison's shoulder. 'Hey, Alison,
pleased you decided to join us?'

Alison made herself laugh up at him. 'Of course! I'm
having a wonderful time.'

'I'm glad you're here.'

'Yes, well, I'm glad too.'

His arm tightened around her, and she felt her body
grow rigid.

'Relax,' said Brian. 'Enjoy yourself.'

She tried very hard to relax against him, but when he
dropped a light kiss on her cheek, a wave of nausea en-
gulfed her. Fortunately she managed to withdraw from
him tactfully, with the excuse that she was going to get
herself something to eat.

Eventually the party progressed from Brian's cabin to
the swimming pool. Unlike Alison, the other counsellors had their swimming costumes and towels with
them.

'I should have thought of telling you to bring your
things,' said Mary. 'Why don't you go and fetch them
from your cabin?'

Because Clint would probably be waiting for her there at this very moment.

'I don't think so.' Alison had the beginnings of a headache. 'I think I'll just sit at the side of the pool and watch.'

Brian overheard her. 'If you skinny-dip, I will too. Go on, Alison, be a sport! Come and skinny-dip with me.'

Laughing, she declined. Her face muscles ached with all the forced laughing she'd done that night.

But Brian and Gary, naturally high-spirited and a little drunk with excitement, were not content to leave it at that. Before she knew what was happening, they had lifted her, Brian holding her arms, Gary her legs, and had thrown her into the pool fully dressed.

When she came up, spluttering but unhurt, she was no longer laughing. All she wanted was to go to bed. But the boys had other ideas. Brian dived down in the water, and inserted his head and neck between her thighs. When he straightened, Alison was straddling his shoulders.

Gary followed suit with a willing Laurie. Someone produced two tennis balls, and a game started, with Brian throwing to Laurie, and Gary throwing to Alison. The trick was to keep the two balls from colliding. But collide they did, of course, accompanied by a great deal of splashing and merriment as the young men lunged to retrieve the balls, and the two girls struggled to retain their balance.

Alison's head was throbbing really hard by this time. She had laughed far too much in the last hour, and if the other three were enjoying the exuberant horseplay, she only wanted it to end. The problem was that, largely through her own doing, she had got herself into this situation, and without seeming to be an utter spoilsport, she didn't know how to get out of it.

With the appearance of a tall figure at the side of the pool, the game ended suddenly. Clint, in black trousers and a black sweater, tall, sleek and as dangerous-looking as a panther, his expression as grim as Alison had ever seen it.

There might have been nobody else in the pool but Alison, for his gaze, stark with disapproval and distaste, was directed solely at her. Chin lifting, she stared back at him. Inside her a spasm of fear tightened her muscles, but outwardly she was defiant.

Brian was the first to break the silence. 'We were just having a party.' He sounded very young, very awkward.

'So I see.' Clint's voice was terse.

'We didn't think we were doing any harm.'

'You weren't—until things began to get out of hand. Did you realise that the campers might hear the noise and arrive to join in the game?'

'We got a bit carried away...' Gary was apologetic.

But Alison, defiant to the last, threw the tennis ball she was holding hard at Gary. The young counsellor, caught off guard and made nervous by Clint's disapproving presence, missed the ball, so that it hit the water with a loud splash.

'We were just having a bit of fun.' Alison's voice came across the pool, high and clear.

'Fun?' Clint's expression did not change.

'Yes, fun. There's nothing wrong with that, is there, Clint?'

'I think we should call it a night.' Mary spoke for the first time. There was a compassionate note in her voice which Alison was far too overwrought to notice.

'Yes, let's.' Wendy, Laurie and Patricia were as eager as Mary to leave the pool.

Laurie slid off Gary's shoulders, but Alison remained where she was, straddling Brian. Clint was still looking at her, the grim expression in his face as sharp as if it had been etched into his skin with a knife.

Beneath Alison, Brian was growing restless. His hands were at her feet, pushing at them, telling her wordlessly to get off him.

'It seems the game is over,' she said brittly. Then she levered herself unhurriedly away from Brian and swam to the edge of the pool.

The counsellors said quiet goodnights to Clint and to each other, before going to their cabins. Alison walked away without a backward glance at Clint.

Her bravado lasted just long enough for her to reach her cabin. Shivering with cold and pain, she dropped on to her bed and closed her eyes. So severe was her headache by this time that she thought her head would burst open. She felt utterly drained; she didn't even have the strength to shed her soaking clothes.

She did not hear the door when it was quietly opened. Not till Clint said, 'Well, Alison,' did she realise he was in the cabin.

Her eyes snapped open in alarm as she pushed herself to a sitting position. 'Clint!' she exclaimed.

'Alison,' he mocked.

It took the little strength she had left to say, 'What are you doing here?'

His eyes glinted. 'You knew I'd come.'

She put a hand to her aching head. 'I wish you'd go away.'

'Oh, no, my darling Alison. Not just yet.' There was infinite danger in his voice.

'I'm very tired,' she protested.

'You didn't look in the least bit tired when I saw you sitting on Brian's shoulders.'

'I am now.' Somehow she managed to keep a sob from her voice. 'Whatever you've come for... Clint, I know you're angry, but can't it wait?'

'It can't, and you know it.' His voice was like a whip, lashing her. 'As for being angry, you and I had a date tonight, Alison.'

'Yes...'

'Why weren't you here? You knew I was coming.

'I changed my mind.'

'And decided to go to Brian's party instead?'

'Yes.' She threw him her steadiest look. 'There's nothing wrong with the counsellors having a party. They've had them in other years.'

'That's true, but this one was getting rowdy.'

'You were only angry because I was there.'

'That, too. We did have a date.' Three quick steps took him to the bed. He towered over her, so that she wished she had thought to stand up the moment she'd seen him. 'What happened to change your mind?'

'The party sounded like fun,' she said lightly.

'That word again!' he snapped. 'You could have had fun with me tonight, Alison, you knew that. Did you think you'd have more fun with Brian?'

Briefly she closed her eyes. She wanted him so much. Even with the pain in her head, that was the one thing that had not changed. She wanted him to hold her, to comfort her, to kiss her.

'Not *more* fun, maybe,' she tried to smile, 'just different.'

'You little tease!' His body was rigid, his face a cold mask of anger.

Alison made a great effort to keep her tone light. 'You're making such a big deal of it. Have *you* never changed your mind, Clint?'

Something moved in his jaw. 'If I make a date with a woman, I don't stand her up so that I can have a good time with someone else.'

Did he have a good time with Virginia on the nights when he was not with Alison? There was a time when she would have told herself she did not care what he did. Now she knew that she'd been fooling herself all the time. She cared far too much.

'I should have told you I was going to Brian's party,' she conceded.

'Damn right, you should have.'

'I'm sorry...' Her voice shook.

'Sorry?' he mocked. 'You don't know what the word means. What are you going to do now, Alison?'

'It's a little late to go up the mountain. I just want to go to bed.' Pointedly, she looked at the door. 'So if you would please go...'

'And leave you to spend the rest of the night tossing and turning in frustration?' His voice was laced with contempt. 'I interrupted the party before you could have your fun with Brian.'

'Clint...' She was beginning to feel very agitated all of a sudden.

'The least I can do is give you some fun of my own.'

'No!' She drew back in alarm. This angry, dangerous Clint was a man she did not know. 'Don't touch me!'

'I'm not asking permission.'

So saying, he pushed her down on the bed and covered her wet body with his. Alison tried her best to evade him as his head came down, but his hands laced themselves in her hair, holding her still.

He began to kiss her then—savage kisses, with no tenderness in them, their only purpose to punish. His tongue probed her lips, seeking to part them, but she kept them tightly closed. He was kissing her so hard that she could feel his teeth against her mouth.

At length he lifted his head. 'Is this the fun you were after?'

'No! I hate it! And I hate you!' she shouted.

'Don't give me that. You enjoy playing hard to get, but you're a passionate woman, Alison. We both know that.'

'Not this kind of passion. Get out of here, Clint! Just get out and leave me alone!'

He moved on top of her, his body heavy against her. Inside her, Alison felt the stirrings of the familiar excitement. But stronger than the excitement was a mingling of anger and grief. She hated the brutal, uncaring way he was treating her.

And then he lifted himself a little away from her, and she took her chance and slapped him hard across his face.

Clint drew a shocked, hissing breath. 'You little hellcat!'

'What about you?' Alison threw the words at him. 'What were you going to do? Rape me?'

A shudder went through his body. 'Is that what you think?'

'The way you're behaving, what do you expect me to think?'

The long body rolled away from her. 'I told you once that I would never force myself on to you, but just now I came close—too damn close!' His voice was harsh, his breathing ragged.

She waited, scarcely breathing.

Abruptly, Clint got off the bed and stood up. When he spoke again, his voice was flat. 'If I hurt you, I'm sorry. I've never forced any woman into sex, I don't intend to begin now. Not even with a little tease like you.'

'Please leave me now, Clint.' Tears were filling her throat and her eyes, and she was determined not to cry in front of him.

'I'm going. As for you, Alison, you're an utter mess. I advise you to get out of those soaking clothes and into bed.'

She remained lying on the bed, just as he'd left her, and watched him go. His body was rigid, all the way from his feet to the muscles bunched in his throat. He left her without a word or a backward glance, and she made no move to call him back.

At the first grey light of dawn Alison donned trousers and a thick blue angora sweater, and walked out of her cabin.

It would be a while before the campers began to wake up. Mist hung low over the mountains, so that only the foothills of the great escarpment were visible, and the grass was wet underfoot. The air was fresh and filled with the fragrant scents of wild shrubs and flowers. A small rock rabbit, looking cold and forlorn, scuttled into the bush at Alison's approach.

It was all so beautiful. She would miss it so much when she left.

She knocked at the door of Clint's cabin, and heard the sound echo in the stillness.

'Come in.'

Clint was already up. He looked as if he had showered and shaved, and he was sitting at a table, writing.

If he was surprised to see her, his expression gave nothing away. 'Good morning, Alison. Isn't this a little early for a social visit?'

'It's not a social visit, Clint.'

Intent eyes regarded her watchfully. 'Oh?'

'I've come to give you my notice.' And, when he did not answer, 'I'm leaving Bushveld, Clint.'

'You're doing no such thing.'

She stared at him, a little wild-eyed. 'You must have anticipated it.'

'With you, Alison, I'm learning never to anticipate anything.'

'Look,' she said unsteadily, 'I can't take any more of this sparring. I just wanted to tell you that I'm leaving. I'll ask Brian or Gary to drive me to the station.'

'You're going nowhere.'

'But, Clint...'

A lithe movement brought him to his feet. 'You think you can just walk out of your job on a moment's whim? You made a commitment when you came here.'

'I can't stay...' she began.

'I'm sorry you feel that way, because you're going to stick it out to the end.'

'You can't stop me going, Clint.'

'Perhaps not,' he agreed smoothly. 'But I can make sure that you never get another job—anywhere.'

She was shocked. 'That's blackmail!' she protested.

'Call it whatever you like.'

'If you won't accept my resignation, I'll go to Virginia.'

'It won't make any difference.'

'She's in charge of the camp. And you never go against her.' Alison said the last words sarcastically.

'We've been over that, Alison, so we don't need to discuss it again now. The fact is, in the final analysis Virginia is still answerable to me. She will not accept your resignation because I won't allow her to.'

Wordlessly, Alison looked at him. At that moment she felt totally helpless.

At length she said, 'I can't remain here, you must know that.'

'Why not?'

'Because after what happened last night I can't bear to see you. I can't even stand the thought of being in the camp at the same time as you.'

Clint's eyes were bleak, but his voice did not change. 'You won't have to worry about that.'

'I don't understand . . . I mean, we can't help running into each other all the time.'

'I'm leaving Bushveld myself this morning,' he told her.

'Wh . . . Where are you going?' Her lips were suddenly stiff.

'The hotels. Something's come up, and I'm needed.'

'How long will you be away?'

He laughed mirthlessly. 'Long enough to make you happy, Alison.'

But Clint could not know what would make her happy. At this moment, she scarcely knew herself.

'Why didn't you tell me before?' Her voice shook.

'I was going to tell you about it—among other things.' His expression was unreadable.

'When?'

'Last night, on the mountain.'

Pain knifed her, sharp and agonising, but she kept her head high, not wanting Clint to know how she felt.

'Well, that's that, then, I suppose,' she said.

Blindly, she turned and walked out of the cabin. She did not see the pain in Clint's eyes as he watched her go.

CHAPTER NINE

ALISON missed Clint more than she could ever have dreamed. Every day she wondered whether she would hear from him. Notwithstanding the disaster of Brian's party, there could be a letter or a phone call. But there was nothing, which seemed to confirm that Alison's feelings were purely one-sided.

While Clint was gone the camp continued to function smoothly under Virginia's direction. From counsellors to campers, everyone seemed to be enjoying themselves.

Even Timmy was happy. His face was tanned and freckled now, and he was a far cry from the pale, frightened little boy who had arrived at Bushveld that first day. He had made friends with some of the other children, but Alison was still his favourite person in the camp. He spent as much time with her as he could, helping her groom the horses, and sneaking extra rides from her when he could.

There had been a letter from Timmy's mother. She was out of the hospital, and his father would be released soon. This was wonderful news indeed, and contributed immensely to Timmy's state of mind.

There was only one thing the little boy seemed to need to make his happiness complete. He wanted to go on a trail-ride. He was becoming so obsessed with the idea that he talked of it constantly. The short rides the other children of his group enjoyed—along the shortish path, with Alison walking beside the horse and holding the rein—were not enough for him.

'Why can't I go on a trail-ride?' he wanted to know.

Alison looked up from the pony she was grooming and laughed. 'Now, how many times have you asked me that question?'

'But why can't I, Alison?'

'Because trail-riding is not for your group, Timmy. You know that.'

'I want to go so badly, Alison. I can ride better than the other kids.'

'That's true,' she agreed.

'Then why?'

'It's the rule.'

'But it's not fair! I can ride, Alison, you know I can.'

Alison did know it. She remembered herself at Timmy's age, galloping over the veld with her father. The hours on her horse had been among the happiest ones of her growing-up years.

Timmy had spent more time with the horses than the sixteen-year-olds. He loved horses dearly, and understood them. A trail-ride would remain in his memory as the highlight of camp.

But Virginia had made herself clear on the subject. Timmy was ten years old, and at Bushveld Camp ten-year-olds did not go on trail-rides.

Privately, Alison agreed with Timmy that Virginia's rule was not fair. A child's ability to cope with a longer ride should be the only factor in deciding who could participate, not the child's age. But she did not undermine Virginia's authority by telling Timmy that.

'Rules are rules,' she said. And then, to distract him, 'My goodness, Timmy, just look at all that dust on

Lady's saddle! Do you think you'd have time to clean it for me?'

With only three days left till the end of camp, Alison went to bed with a heavy heart. There was still no word from Clint. It had never occurred to her that she might leave Bushveld without seeing him again.

She did not know at what point in the night she became aware that someone was in her bed. For a moment she was quite sure she was dreaming.

But the warmth of the long, hard body that had curled itself snugly around hers was no dream. In a second her whole body had grown rigid.

'Clint?' she exclaimed disbelievingly.

'Mm,' grunted a sleepy voice.

'What on earth are you *doing* here?'

There was no answer as Clint curled himself more tightly around her, and an arm went around her, holding her just beneath her breasts. His breathing was slow and steady.

'Are you really asleep, Clint?' she whispered.

'Been travelling all day without a break,' he muttered groggily.

Alison decided to let him go on sleeping, although there would be no more rest for her tonight.

Gripped by a savage joy, she lay quite still within the warm embrace of his body. He was all around her, enveloping her, his thighs and hips against hers, the roughness of his chest against her back.

Gently, so as not to waken him, she took his hand and laid it on her breast. And then she put her own hand over his. Excitement began to fill her body, hot waves of desire flooding through her, one upon the other. Never before in her life had she been quite so desperate to make love as she was now.

It was dawn—and Alison had lain for hours drinking in the seductive maleness of Clint's body—when he stirred. The hand on her breast moved, tightened, the fingers beginning to caress her nipple. She held her breath, wondering if he was still sleeping. And then she felt him throb against her in the beginnings of desire, and she knew he was awake.

'Clint . . .'

His only answer was to nuzzle his lips against the back of her throat.

'What are you doing here?'

'Holding you,' he murmured. 'Dying to make love to you.'

Her heart was racing, and her body felt hot. But she laughed as she said, 'Rascal!' and turned in his arms.

He was so close to her that their noses touched on the pillow. 'When did you get back to camp, Clint?' she asked.

'After midnight. Everyone was asleep.'

'And I suppose you'd mislaid the key to your cabin?'

She knew the answer to that one, but she wanted to hear him say it.

His hands slid beneath the top of her pyjamas. 'Of course not.'

'Then why are you here?' She was finding it harder and harder to breathe.

He was caressing her back now, the erotic touch of his fingers making her blood course like a veld-fire through her veins. 'I wanted to be with you.'

'And so you just walked straight in.'

With his tongue, he traced a line around her lips. 'As you see.'

Alison's heart was pounding so hard in her chest that she thought he must hear it. It was a double pounding because she could feel the beat of his heart as well as her own. 'You never thought to ask?'

'You were asleep. Can you imagine sleeping together every night, Alison?'

Every night until the end of camp must be what he meant. But there were so few nights left to them.

'You could have woken me...' she began.

'I enjoyed watching you sleep. Besides, the last time we met—after that wretched party of Brian's—you were so insistent that you never wanted to set eyes on me again.'

'That was a long time ago,' she said unsteadily.

'Did you mean what you said then?'

'I... At the time I did.'

'And now, Alison?' His voice was suddenly husky.

And she was able to say, 'Not now. Clint, I'm so sorry about what happened that night.'

He whispered against her mouth, 'No sorrier than I am for my own part in it.'

'I should have told you I'd changed my plans.'

'Even if you had told me, chances are I'd have been just as angry. I wanted you to come up the mountain with me that night.'

'Clint...'

'Alison, it's over.'

'Do you mean that?' she asked incredulously.

'I don't know why you went to the party, but I'd be happy if we could put it behind us. Forget the whole thing ever happened.' He was looking at her. 'I'm willing to, if you are, Alison.'

'Yes,' she whispered. It was hard to believe that he would make it so easy for her.

'Do you know how beautiful you are when you sleep?' he asked, so close to her that he seemed to be breathing the words between her lips.

'You could tell me.'

Laughter bubbled in his throat, as his hands moved downwards, shaping themselves to her hips, her buttocks, the tops of her thighs. 'I'm telling you all the time, Alison, in my own way. Don't you know that?'

What did she know? That he desired her. That she desired him. That their bodies called out to each other, ached for each other. Oh, yes, she knew that. But did he love her?

'And you, Alison, what are you telling me?'

She was confused. 'What do you mean?'

'When I woke up, I found my hand on your breast.'

She moved against him. 'Yes.'

'Do you know what it does to me when you move like that?' Clint groaned, and pulled her closer against him. 'Alison, I don't remember putting my hand on your breast before I went to sleep.'

'You didn't,' she whispered.

'Did you put it there?' His breathing had quickened.

'Yes . . .'

'Does that mean you were glad to find me in your bed?'

It was not possible for her to be coy with him. They had gone too far for that, and coyness had never been her scene, anyway. Besides, her warm body must give him all the answers he wanted.

'Yes, I was glad.'

Bending over her, he cupped her head in his hands so that he could kiss her, and after a moment she was kissing him too—long, hungry kisses, as if they were trying to make up for all the time they had been apart. They touched each other's bodies with their hands, caressing all the while that they were kissing. Clint's passions called forth an answering passion deep inside Alison, so that nothing mattered save for her body's urgent response to his. His lips and tongue brushed her throat and the soft swell of her breasts, creating trails of fire wherever they touched her warm, sensitive skin. And Alison, passion making her abandoned, let her hands move over him, her fingers seeking the hardness of his shoulders and sliding over the roughness of his chest.

But after a while Clint lifted his head. 'I missed you so much.' His voice was rough.

She looked back at him. 'You never wrote to me, never phoned.'

Uncharacteristically, he hesitated before saying, 'No.'

'Because of the fight we had after Brian's party?'

'No, it wasn't that.'

'Then why not? You could have been in touch, Clint.'

'Yes, I could,' he agreed.

'But you decided not to.' All the pent-up longing, the doubts and fears, turned to anger. 'Now you have the nerve to say that you missed me!'

'I did.'

'I don't know whether to believe you.'

'Are we having another fight, Alison?'

'If that's what you want to call it,' she said hotly. 'Were you having such a good time while you were away that you forgot I existed?'

'This isn't the girl I left behind,' drawled Clint after a long moment. 'The girl who didn't want to care about anyone else. Does this mean you've changed, Alison?'

She couldn't trust herself to answer the question. Instead, as calmly as she could, she said, 'I just wonder why you didn't bother to be in touch.'

'There was a reason, Alison.'

'Was there really?'

'Yes, darling. And in my own time I'll tell it to you. Can you trust me till then?'

I'd trust you with my life, she thought, and wondered whether the endearment meant anything.

'I think so.'

'And I think we're talking a darn sight too much.'

With one lithe movement he pulled her across him, so that she was lying on top of him. One of her legs slid between his, and her arms went around his neck. And then Clint kissed her until she was almost insane with pleasure.

The first sounds of morning were beginning to filter through into the cabin, but Alison hardly heard them. She and Clint had never shared an intimacy quite like this. His legs had wrapped themselves around hers, so that she could feel the throb of his desire against her. It was at the same time frightening and exciting to know that she had such power to arouse the man she loved.

We fit together, she thought exultantly. Our bodies were made for each other. What we do together is right and lovely. It's the way it was meant to be.

She started when there was a quick rap on the door, and a voice called, 'Alison, wake up!'

Alison stiffened in Clint's arms. 'Mary,' she whispered against his ear.

'Alison! Are you awake? Time for breakfast!'

'Better answer her,' Clint advised quietly.

'Go on without me,' she called back. 'I'll see you in a few minutes.'

Clint gave a ragged laugh as Mary walked away. 'You've just been granted your reprieve,' he said.

'Reprieve?' Her voice was choked.

'We can hardly make love now, not when you're expected to show yourself at breakfast.' He pushed himself a little away from her, so that he could look down into her eyes. 'I wonder if you would have let me make love to you, Alison?'

She looked back at him wordlessly. Her body was on fire, the emotions that raged inside her like nothing she had ever known. She wanted to speak, but her mouth was so dry that the words did not make it past her lips.

'I'm a normal man, Alison, and I can't take this suspense much longer. More than anything in the world I want to make love to you. I'd like to stay with you all day.'

'I know...'

'But it's not fated to be.' With an obvious effort, he pushed himself away from her.

'No.' She was beyond saying anything more than the simplest words.

'I'll come and see you again tonight, Alison.'

'All right,' she whispered.

Clint pulled her to him for a final kiss. 'No partying with Brian tonight,' he warned. 'I can't answer for what will happen if you're not here!'

Breakfast was almost over when Clint walked into the big meal tent. He had showered and shaved and changed his clothes since Alison had seen him, and despite the fact that he'd had little sleep, he looked fresh and rested.

Virginia officially welcomed Clint back to camp. He made jokes with the children and friendly conversation with the counsellors, catching up on all the news that had happened in his absence. There were even a few innocuous remarks to Alison.

Alison moved through the day in a kind of glow. While she worked with the horses, and took the older campers for a ride through the foothills, her mind was on Clint.

When Timmy began his daily pleading to go on a trailride, she smiled at him. 'We've been over this, honey,' she reminded him.

'Camp will be over in a few days. I want to go so badly, Alison!'

'I know you do.'

'The older kids went on a special ride today—I heard them talking. Can't I just go on one small ride of my own?'

The eyes were as big and as eloquent as ever. Alison always found herself smiling whenever she looked at Timmy. Even now that he was over his accident, and feeling happier about his parents, there was something about the little boy that endeared itself to her.

'Virginia wouldn't like it,' she pointed out.

'She wouldn't have to know.'

He was a difficult child to refuse. Besides, he really wasn't asking for much. He was good with horses, and she knew he could cope with a ride. The fact that Virginia's rules were unreasonable wasn't Timmy's fault.

It was partly her relaxed and happy state, partly the fact that camp was almost over, that finally led Alison to give in. Would it really be so wrong to let Timmy have he one thing that he would remember long after camp ad ended? Virginia need never know about it.

Timmy was quite ecstatic as Alison saddled up two orses. She smiled as she watched how confidently he nounted the smaller one. He was bubbling with enthusi- sm as they left the paddock and walked the horses in he direction of one of the easier trails.

All the way he chatted happily. Watching how well he andled the horse and himself, Alison was glad she had iven him the one thing he'd longed for so much. Timmy vas as at home on a horse as she had been at his age. here were rules that were meant to be broken, and in reaking this one no harm would be done to anyone.

They were almost back at camp when it happened. A nake slithered across the path. Alison saw it in time, nd managed to control her rearing horse. She shouted warning to Timmy, but it was too late. Timmy's horse ad reared as well. Timmy, caught off his guard, fell to he ground as the horse galloped away in the direction f the stables.

'Timmy!' Alison had leaped from her horse in a econd and was kneeling beside the child. Her heart was n her throat as she saw his awkward, twisted position n the ground. 'Timmy, honey, are you all right?'

He grimaced up at her from the ground. 'My leg feels unny.'

She made an effort to control her panic. 'The leg that vas broken in the motor accident?'

'Yes.' He was trying very hard not to cry.

'Do you think you can walk, honey?'

He shifted position. 'I don't know.'

'Don't even try.' Alison put her arm around him. 'I'm oing to carry you back on my horse.'

His mouth was trembling. 'Virginia's gonna be angry.'

'Let's not think about Virginia now,' Alison said grimly. 'The important thing is to see that you're OK.'

But there would be hell to pay when Virginia found out what had happened, Alison knew. Which happened almost immediately. When a couple of campers saw Alison riding into the camp grounds, holding Timmy in her arms, they ran to tell Virginia. By the time Alison reached the stables she was met by a reception committee comprised of Virginia and Clint and a gathering of children.

Clint took Timmy out of Alison's arms. Alison tried to speak, but Virginia silenced her with a grim, 'Later.' It was a tense and silent group that made its way to the sick-bay.

Only when the door had been closed on the interested campers did Virginia speak. 'You took Timmy on a ride—against my orders!'

'I nagged her,' Timmy began, but Alison interrupted him.

'It was my own idea,' she said tersely. 'Look, I know I was wrong, but before we talk about that, please can we see if Timmy is all right?'

'Yes,' said Clint, who was bending over the little boy. 'Same leg, Timmy?'

'Yes.'

'We'd better have it seen to.'

The child looked scared. 'I don't want to go to hospital.'

Clint put his hand on his shoulder. 'We'll have to drive into town and see a doctor,' he told him.

Seeing the fear in Timmy's eyes, Alison said, 'Couldn' we let Wendy have a look at him first?' Besides being a counsellor, Wendy was also a registered nurse, and she looked after the usual minor ailments in the sick-bay.

'How typical of your irresponsible attitude, Alison!' snapped Virginia. 'Don't you realise this could be serious?'

Clint's eyes met Alison's. 'In view of the fact that the leg was broken previously, I don't think we should waste any time. I really think it's necessary for a doctor to see Timmy.'

'Yes, of course.' Alison forbore to point out that her suggestion that Wendy look at Timmy's leg first had been made only because the little boy looked so petrified.

'I'll come, too,' said Alison.

'You've done enough damage for one day,' said Virginia.

'I'd really like to go, Clint.' Alison threw the man she loved a look of appeal. 'I feel so bad about what happened. And I want to...'

But Virginia stopped her coolly. 'I'll go with Clint and Timmy. As for you, Alison, I'm sure you have work to do. I suggest you get back to it.'

Alison's eyes went once more to the man who just a few hours earlier had been in her bed, but the look he gave back to her was impersonal. 'It's better this way,' was all he said.

'Look,' said Alison, a little desperately, 'I'm so dreadfully sorry this happened. It was a freak accident—a snake frightened the horses.'

'It's a rule that children of Timmy's age don't go on trail-rides.' Virginia's voice was icy, and Alison sensed that she was restraining herself, that if it were not for the little boy's presence in the room she would be saying a lot more.

'I know that,' said Alison. 'The thing is, I think an older child would have been thrown too, in the circumstances.'

'An older child is stronger and more competent.'

'Timmy *is* competent. I wish I could make you understand, Virginia. You see...'

'I understand that you decided to do what you wanted. This camp has been one of our best—no accidents, no mishaps of any kind, a spotless record until now. And with three days to go you've ruined it! All along, you and Timmy...' Virginia glanced at the boy and stopped. Perhaps she realised that she had already said too much in his presence.

'Instead of going on with this discussion,' Clint put in briskly, 'let's get Timmy seen to. Come on, old fellow.'

So saying, he lifted the little boy in his arms and walked out of the sick-bay. Alison followed them, hungering for a tender look, some comforting word.

But at the car she felt suddenly helpless. She looked at Clint, then at Virginia beside him. In the end, all she could do was give Timmy a quick, reassuring hug.

To Clint, there was nothing she could say.

CHAPTER TEN

THE NEXT few hours were the unhappiest Alison had spent at Bushveld. Her thoughts kept going to Timmy. Although she knew that the accident could have happened to anyone, still she blamed herself for it. If only she had remained steadfast in the face of the little boy's pleading, nothing would have happened to him. The fact that it was his recently injured leg which he had fallen on was a particular cause for anxiety.

If only Clint would phone and let her know about the child! But the hours passed, and by the time the evening *braaivleis* had ended, and campers and counsellors had retired to their cabins, there had still been no word from him. It occurred to her that when Clint did get back, he would probably go straight to his cabin, and she would have to wait until morning to find out about Timmy.

It was quite late when there was a knock at Alison's door. She ran to open it.

'Clint! Oh, Clint, I didn't think you'd still be coming!' she exclaimed.

He stood still a moment, taking in her distraught expression. Something moved in his eyes, but she was in no state to notice it.

Then he said, 'Why not, Alison? I told you this morning that I'd come.'

'Yes, I know. But that was before... Clint, how's Timmy? Where is he?'

157

'He's fine.' Incredibly, he was smiling. 'He's gone to bed. We got back to camp about fifteen minutes ago, and I've just left him in his cabin. He's probably asleep by now.'

'Oh, Clint...' Alison felt weak with relief, 'I've been so anxious!'

'I knew you would be. I tried several times to phone you from town, but for some reason I couldn't get through to Bushveld. And on the road coming back we only passed one phone-booth, and the phone was out of order.'

Alison pushed a hand through her hair. 'I didn't know what to think... I was sure something really dreadful had happened to Timmy.'

'No, Alison, he's fine.'

'Virginia was right, I suppose,' she said ruefully. 'I shouldn't have let Timmy ride.'

Clint smiled his wonderful devil-may-care smile that Alison had thought never to see again. 'You gave that young man his best day at camp,' he told her.

Alison drew in her breath. *Really?*

'Really.' Clint was laughing as he dropped his long body into a chair, and motioned to Alison. 'Come and sit on my lap while I tell you about it.'

There was nothing she wanted more.

For as long as she could she sat quite still, savouring the hardness of his thighs beneath her, the strength of the arms that circled her, feeling the beat of his heart against her chest, her own heart beating faster when his lips moved in her hair.

She didn't feel like talking, but there were things she had to know. 'Tell me about Timmy,' she invited.

'Because of the previous injury, the doctor sent us to the nearest hospital for X-rays. You'll be glad to know the leg was just bruised.'

Alison expelled a tense breath. 'Oh, thank God! You don't know how I worried. I kept blaming myself.'

'Needlessly. It was in fact a freak accident. There are snakes in the veld, and they scare the hell out of the horses. It could have happened to anyone.'

Alison tilted her head back to look at him. 'That's not what you said this morning. Actually, you didn't say anything—you just looked so grim. Why didn't you stand up for me, Clint?'

'Put yourself in my position, darling,' he said, and tucked her head firmly back where it belonged against his shoulder. 'I was as worried as you were about Timmy. I knew we had to get him to a doctor. And you'd deliberately gone against Virginia.' She felt the laughter bubbling in his throat as he added, 'Again.'

'So you do think I was wrong...'

'I don't.'

'Are you saying I was *right*?'

'Not entirely.' Clint was laughing again. 'You were wrong to break a rule of the camp.'

'But?' She could hear that there was a 'but' in it somewhere.

'You did the right thing for Timmy. Guess what his first words were when we left the hospital? He wanted to know if he could ride again tomorrow. He said the trail-ride was the best thing that had happened to him in camp. You gave that little boy the happiest time he's had since the motor accident.'

'Then you don't *mind* that I defied Virginia?'

'I suppose I wish it hadn't been necessary.' He put a hand through her tumbled hair, stroking it away from her forehead. 'I wish you and Virginia had the same way of looking at things, but you don't. You explained it to me yourself after one of your set-tos. Virginia is methodical and efficient; she lives by learned theories and concepts. You let your emotions rule your head every time.'

'And break all the rules in doing so.'

'Yes. But then, some rules deserve to be broken. For Timmy, your way has been the better one all along.'

She snuggled closer against him. 'I want to see him,' she said.

'Tomorrow.' Clint's voice had changed. When he spoke again, there was a new tone in his voice. 'When you saw me tonight, you seemed surprised.'

'Yes...'

'Why, Alison?'

'I didn't think you'd come,' she confessed.

'Why not?'

He sounded so serious all at once that she was bewildered. 'I've already told you the reason.'

'I want to hear it again.'

'Things had changed. There was Timmy—the accident... You seemed so angry with me.'

'People do get angry, Alison. Even people who mean a great deal to each other. It's the way life is. But anger doesn't have to change the things that matter.'

'Maybe not,' she sighed.

'I was angry the night I came to your cabin and found you'd gone to Brian's party. But we got over that.'

Something was tightening inside her. 'You're trying to tell me something.'

'It's true I was upset about Timmy. But it didn't change what you and I have together, Alison.'

What *do* we have? I love you. But do you feel anything more than physical desire for me? she thought.

'I didn't know what to expect,' she admitted.

'You were thinking of Raymond.'

'Yes.' She swallowed hard on a throat that was suddenly dry. 'It's true I was thinking of him. Things went wrong after we argued, after he was angry.'

'I believe things went wrong long before that,' Clint said quietly. 'I believe Raymond realised before you did that what you had all along was a sister-brother relationship.'

'You could be right.' Alison was on the verge of tears.

'The way Raymond went about things was wrong,' Clint went on. 'He should have told you about his feelings—about Edna. But maybe he didn't have the courage to tell you.'

Her lips quivered. 'Do we have to talk about Raymond now?'

'Yes. Because you have to understand that I'm not Raymond. Don't you know that yet, Alison?'

'I think I do.' Her voice was choked.

'Well, that's good.' His voice changed. 'Do you know we're talking a darn sight too much? That's not what I came here for.'

The words sent a hot current of feeling rushing through her. Putting her arm around his neck, she whispered, 'Kiss me, Clint.'

He made a sound in his throat. 'What do you think I've been wanting to do ever since I left you this morning?'

Their first kisses were as tantalising as always—playful stroking around the corners of lips, a nibbling of earlobes, playful but intoxicating, kindling the desire for much more.

But within minutes the tenor of their kisses began to change. There was passion in their lips now, hunger and possessiveness, and the need to explore the sweetness of each other's mouths. There was a fiercely joyous meeting of lips and tongues and teeth, while at the same time their hands began to move over each other.

'You're so lovely,' Clint said once, when they drew apart to take breath.

'Am I?' Alison wanted to hear him say it—as often as possible.

'The loveliest thing that ever happened to me. Beautiful, sexy, desirable—you're all those things, Alison.'

'You're lovely, too.' It was as much as she had ever allowed herself to say. Pushing her fingers into the opening of his shirt, she slid her hands, flat-palmed, over his chest.

'Provocative as well!' His breath hissed in his throat, and his voice was ragged. 'A beautiful and provocative little siren, luring me the way the mermaids used to do.'

'Not the first time you've called me a mermaid. Where do I lure you to?' she asked against his lips.

'To the greatest joys, darling.'

Which was where he was taking her. As he pushed the pyjama top from her shoulders and began to make love to her breasts, touching and kissing alternately, her nipples hardened into his fingers, and she thought she would go crazy with pleasure.

Somehow Clint seemed to know all the most sensitive areas of her body. The little hollow at the base of her throat, the soft skin beneath her earlobes. The palms of her hands and the delicate soles of her feet. Teasing strokes of a rough tongue sent shudder after shudder through her system. She ached to have his lips return to hers, so that their kisses could be mutual ones.

At length, Alison could stand it no longer, and she buried her hands in his hair and guided his head back to her mouth. The warm hiss of his breath blew between her lips, then he was kissing her again—and she him—with all the passion that was in them both. There was a fierceness in their kisses, but a sweetness too, like nothing she had ever known, so that all she wanted was for the kissing to go on and on for ever.

She felt dizzy when Clint raised his head and looked down at her. And then he lifted her in his arms and carried her to the bed. As if she were a bride being carried over the threshold, was her involuntary thought.

She began to tremble as he undressed her. Finally she was naked, and now it was his eyes that were making love to her body. There was something very akin to worship in them as they moved over her—over her soft breasts, the nipples pink and hard with desire, her hips, slender yet seductively rounded, and the long, shapely legs.

He removed his outer clothes, keeping on only his underwear as he lay down beside her on the bed. Their arms went around each other, each seeking to be as close to the other as possible. Long, hard male body against the soft female one, in a closeness that was such a heady onslaught on Alison's senses that her hunger, already intense, was fanned to a flame that was almost unbearable.

A small moan of pleasure escaped her as they lay facing each other, thigh to thigh and hip to hip, and began to kiss once more. Clint's hands were moving over her, shaping themselves to the soft mounds of her buttocks, then sliding between their two bodies to caress her nipples again.

'I want so much to make love to you, Alison,' he said at last, his voice husky. 'Properly, the way a man makes love to a woman. But I don't know if you're ready for it.'

She couldn't have said why she was shy suddenly, so that she stiffened in his arms. Perhaps it was because she had never made love with a man, and, though she loved Clint and wanted him to make love to her, she felt suddenly tremulous. And so terribly vulnerable—for he had never said that he loved her. If he had, it might have been different.

The moment of indecision got through to him. 'You have to be ready for this,' he said raggedly. 'Otherwise there's no point.'

'Perhaps I am ready,' she whispered.

'You have to be sure.'

'Perhaps I am,' she said again.

'That's not good enough.'

'Clint . . .'

'It's important that there should be no regrets later.' With an obvious effort, he pushed himself away from her. 'God, Alison, you don't know what it does to me to leave you—but in the long run it's better for us both if I don't take what you're offering.'

Nerves raw, she watched him dress. She wanted to stop him, to draw him back to her, but some inner hesitation, even now, kept her lying where she was.

In the doorway, he stopped and looked back at her. 'When you're certain you're ready, tell me, darling. I'll be waiting for you.'

Alison lay for hours, just as he had left her, aching with the frustration of having been left unfulfilled, trying to ignore the pain that came with the knowledge that camp was ending and that she would not see him again after that.

She loved him so much. She had never dreamed that it was possible for her to love a man as much as she loved Clint. It was a love she had tried so hard to fight, but the battle had been unequal from the start. And he would never know it.

But he could! It was already morning when she sat up suddenly, struck by an electrifying thought.

'When you're certain you're ready, tell me,' he'd said.

Well, she *was* ready to make love with Clint, and she would tell him so. They could make love tonight—one glorious night that she would always have to remember. She would tell him also that she loved him. She had reached the point where she had nothing to lose.

Eagerly, Alison jumped out of bed. After showering, she pulled on the first clothes in sight. She was on her way to Clint's cabin when Brian stopped her with a question. She was walking further when Virginia appeared with an order. Alison answered politely, concealing her impatience.

And then Clint himself came out of his cabin, only to be waylaid by a group of campers. Alison pushed a hand through her hair and smiled wryly.

Things were going to be hectic today, for the campers were leaving. By tonight, only the counsellors would be left. They were going to the hotel to dine and dance and have a farewell party. By tomorrow, most of them would be gone. Alison would have to wait until after the party for her chance to be alone with Clint.

The day got off to a hectic start. With seventy children packing their things and getting ready to go, the counsellors were kept busy. The older campers were able to do their own packing, the younger children had to be helped. Inevitably, possessions were missing and had to be found. New arrangements had to be made. Even with Virginia's expert organisation, there was a lot to do.

There was a flurry of goodbyes. Addresses were being exchanged. Arrangements were being made for reunions. Some of the campers were going home by train, many were being fetched by their parents.

Towards midday, a car carrying Timmy's parents, and driven by Timmy's uncle, Joe Roscoe, arrived. Timmy had no idea that they were coming, for until the last minute it had not been certain whether his father would be out of hospital in time, and everyone had agreed that it would be a terrible thing for the little boy to be disappointed.

Clint stood talking to the Roscoes while Alison went to call Timmy.

Timmy saw his uncle's car and was going towards it, when suddenly he stopped still. His body went quite rigid, only to begin shuddering a few moments later. Beneath his tan his little face went deathly pale. Watching him, Alison tensed, ready to catch him if he fainted.

Instead he let out a great whooping shout, and then he was running headlong towards his parents, hurtling into their bodies as their arms went around him.

As Timmy started his dash, Alison and Clint moved away from the emotional little group, allowing them to be alone in their reunion.

But a while later Timmy came to Alison. 'Come meet my mum and dad,' he beamed proudly.

'I'd like that very much,' she smiled at him. She was going to miss Timmy.

'So you're Alison. We've heard so much about you in Timmy's letters,' his mother said. She was a slender, pretty woman, with Timmy's smile and eyes.

'Timmy looks wonderful,' said his father, and Alison glimpsed tears in his eyes. Mr Roscoe had been out of hospital only three days, and evidently the reunion with his son had been very emotional for him.

'We were so worried about our son,' Mrs Roscoe told her. 'Timmy really didn't want to go to camp. He was nervous about leaving home to begin with, and then came the accident, and he was so badly shaken by that. And now here he is—so strong and happy. I can't believe it. It's like a miracle!'

'A miracle that Alison must take complete credit for.' Clint, who was back on the scene and had heard the conversation, put a casual arm around her shoulders. 'Timmy's recovery is entirely due to Alison, Mrs Roscoe. We all did our best with him, but Alison was the one who knew what was right for him all along.'

A warm glow spread through Alison's body at Clint's words of praise. It was one thing for her to know that she'd made Timmy happy, another for Clint to acknowledge it publicly.

'I even went on a trail-ride,' Timmy babbled excitedly. 'Can I go to camp again next year, Mom? Dad? And can I go on another trail-ride then, Alison?'

'Timmy, darling, you haven't even asked Alison if she'll be here next year,' his mother protested.

The hand around Alison's shoulder tightened as Clint said, 'She'll be here.'

Alison's eyes flew to his. She would have liked to ask him how he could so confidently predict where she would be a year from now, when she didn't know the answer to that one herself. But there was the strangest look in his eyes, so that she did not ask the question. In front of the Roscoes, it was not the time for it anyway.

Finally it was time for the Roscoes to go. For Alison, the parting was difficult. Timmy clung to her for a long moment, and she had to try very hard to keep her tears at bay.

'Will you write to me, Alison?' he asked.

'Yes, I will, honey.'

'And you *will* be here next year?'

'We'll have to see about that.'

She gave the little boy a warm hug, and even managed a smile as the car drove away.

'That was hard for you,' said Clint, his arm around her shoulder once more.

'Yes, it was. I'm going to miss Timmy. I'll send him a postcard when I get back home.'

If this parting was hard, how was she going to survive the parting with Clint? It was going to be sheerest hell.

'Clint,' she asked, 'why did you let Timmy think I'd be here again next year?'

'Won't you be?'

'Of course not. I'll have my stables by then. I can't possibly be in two places at once.'

'Could be I was mistaken, then.' But he didn't look as if he felt in the least in the wrong. His eyes were sparkling and his grin was so wicked that Alison looked at him suspiciously.

But there was no time to pursue the subject. Another departing family had claimed Clint's attention, and Alison had work to do in the stables.

Gradually, the bustle of activity began to lessen. Most of the campers had left, and those who remained were in the process of leaving. A big van was parked near the games tent, and two men were busy loading into it all the equipment that would be going into storage until next summer. For the counsellors there was work a-plenty. Dinner and dancing at the hotel seemed a long way away.

The sun was already setting when Alison had to go to one of the store-rooms. It was locked, and apparently Clint was the last one seen with the key.

She looked for him everywhere. Finally she decided to try his cabin. She was about to knock at his door when she was caught by a movement at one of the windows.

And then she saw them: Clint and Virginia. Virginia's hands were clasped around Clint's neck, Clint's arms were around Virginia's waist. He was smiling down at her. They were talking, but the window was closed and Alison could not hear what they said.

Alison's feet were rooted to the ground. She was like a statue, frozen, totally incapable of moving.

And then Clint bent his head and kissed Virginia. Pain knifed Alison's chest, and it was like no pain she had ever felt in her life. Briefly she closed her eyes, and for an awful moment she thought she would faint. But mercifully, movement returned to her body a few moments later. She fled the scene without a backward glance.

The van that was being loaded with things for storage was still outside the kitchen tent. Alison spoke to the driver.

Then she ran to her cabin and pulled her suitcase from the top of her cupboard. It didn't take her long to pack. She was like a robot, moving mechanically from drawers to suitcase, doing what she had to do, all the while keeping her emotions tightly in check. If she allowed herself to cry, she might never be able to stop.

Only when she'd finished packing did she go to look for Mary.

Her friend was horrified. 'You can't just leave!'

'I must,' said Alison flatly.

'The farewell party, Alison. The dinner at the hotel...'

'I can't go through with it, I was so sure you'd understand.'

Mary looked distressed. 'Maybe there's an explanation.'

'Yes, there is, and it's simple,' Alison said grimly. 'Clint isn't a one-woman man. Virginia tried to tell me that once, and she was right. I'm the stupid one, to be surprised. I knew from Jenny that they'd been close, and I saw the way things were with them at the hotel that night.'

'That night wasn't a date, Alison. They were just discussing camp business.'

'I know that. But it doesn't change what happened just now.'

'You could try talking to him,' her friend suggested.

'No. Oh, God, Mary, when I think of how close I came to letting him...' Alison paused a moment. On a harsher note, she said, 'I have to get going.'

'Don't go, Alison—not like this,' begged Mary.

'I have to. I really can't face the party. Not after seeing them together.'

'Couldn't you just stay for tonight? Clint doesn't know that you saw him. Nobody need ever know. And tomorrow you could leave with the rest of us.'

'You're asking me to put on a brave face?'

'Something like that.'

Alison considered the idea—but only for a moment. 'I hate the thought of leaving without a word. But I won't be able to pretend tonight—not when I'm tearing apart inside, every nerve, every sinew. And then later...'

'Later?' Mary prompted.

'Clint said he'd come to my cabin after the party.' Her lips quivered. 'You can see why it's better if I leave now. It's not even as if I have any work left to do. God, I was a fool to let myself fall in love, Mary! It's such sheer hell.' She glanced at her watch. 'It's time to go.'

'The last train has already left,' said Mary.

'From our little station, yes. But the van is going into town, and I'll be able to find transport there. I may have to wait a while, and make some connections, but one way or another I'll get home.'

There were tears in Mary's eyes. 'I was hoping you'd be back next year.'

'Isn't it funny, Clint said something of the kind to Timmy,' said Alison sadly. 'Let's make this a quick goodbye, Mary. I don't want to cry.'

They hugged fiercely, and then Alison went to the van with her suitcase. She made sure nobody saw her go.

She stared out of the window as the van left the camp grounds. The highest mountain peaks were still light, but the lower slopes and the valleys and the river were grey and shaded. Once a widow bird flew across the road. For whom was she grieving? Alison wondered.

Somehow she had managed to keep her tears at bay until now, but suddenly it was all too much for her. Not caring what the van-driver thought of her, she put her hands over her eyes and wept.

CHAPTER ELEVEN

THERE WAS nobody at the station to meet Alison's train. Nor had she expected anyone, for as far as her family knew she was only due home the next day.

It had been a long trip back from Bushveld Camp. Alison had been fortunate enough to have a compartment to herself for part of the way, where she could allow herself the luxury of a few more tears. But after a while the train had begun to fill up, and she had dried her eyes and looked unhappily out of the window.

By the time she reached the village she had made at least one decision: she would speak to her father that very evening about acquiring her own stables. He might know if there was something—not too expensive—for sale. If he didn't, Alison would begin to make her own enquiries tomorrow. She would be content to start with something very modest, and gradually she would begin to build it up.

Leaving the dusty station-yard, she was about to walk to the village post office, where she could phone home for a lift, when someone said, 'Alison?' A tentative voice.

She swung round. Raymond was standing not three feet away from her, Edna beside him.

Such a short while ago she would have felt uncomfortable; now she was able to say, quite easily, 'Hello, Raymond . . . Edna . . .'

Raymond had an intensely embarrassed expression on his face. 'I heard you'd been away,' he said awkwardly.

'I've been working at a children's camp in the Drakensberg. I've just come from there.'

He looked down at her luggage. 'Can we give you a lift home?'

'Alison's probably expecting her family to pick her up.' This from Edna. She was standing close at Raymond's side, and now she tucked her left hand possessively through his arm. On the fourth finger sparkled a huge diamond.

She wants me to see the ring, Alison realised. Unexpectedly, she was amused.

'Thanks for the offer,' she said, 'but Edna's right—I know Dad will be around to pick me up.'

'Well, if you're sure...' said Raymond.

'Quite sure.' Alison picked up her suitcase. 'By the way, congratulations to you both on your marriage.'

Raymond looked startled, Edna's eyes were narrowed with suspicion.

After a charged moment, Raymond said, 'Thanks, Alison.'

'I hope you'll be very happy together.'

'We will be,' Edna said firmly, the suspicious look deepening. 'Daddy's given Raymond a marvellous promotion, and we've just bought a house.'

Alison smiled. 'That's wonderful!'

'Alison...' Raymond took a step towards her. 'I hope there are no hard feelings.'

'Raymond!' Edna looked daggers.

'This has to be said.' He was unexpectedly firm. 'Alison and I have been friends all our lives. And I...I'm not proud of the way I behaved.'

'No hard feelings,' she reassured him. 'Not any more. We had fun growing up together, being each other's best friends. That's the part I want to remember.'

'We did have fun.' There was a dazed look in Raymond's eyes.

'Whatever happened afterwards—well, let's not forget what we used to have,' added Alison.

Edna's hand tightened on Raymond's arm. 'You don't have to listen to this,' she said harshly.

'Alison's right, honey—we did have a wonderful friendship.' And to Alison, 'You're very generous.'

Alison smiled at them both. 'I meant what I said—I hope you'll be very happy together.' And she knew that she meant it.

And then, before Raymond could ask her if she had a new love in her own life, she walked away.

Twenty minutes after she had phoned her father, he arrived in his truck to fetch her. He hugged her fiercely. 'It's good to have you back, Alison. We thought you weren't coming till tomorrow.'

Alison managed a smile. 'There was a change of plans.'

The rest of the family were equally delighted to have her home. In no time at all Alison's mother had whipped up a meal, and they all sat together in the big kitchen, eating and catching up on one another's news.

Alison told them about camp—about Timmy, about the counsellors and the horses and the trail-rides. Not a word about Clint.

'Your employer... Mr Demaine. What was he like?' her mother asked at length.

'Very nice.' Through her pain, Alison tried to speak the words lightly. She saw Lynn give her a thoughtful look.

'I thought he would be,' said her mother. 'So good-looking, but with an honest, open face. I liked him.'

Alison knew she had to change the subject. 'The counsellors were nice, too. One in particular—Mary. We became very friendly.'

'Mary!' exclaimed her mother. 'How stupid of me, I almost forgot. A girl called Mary phoned—she wanted to speak to you.'

'Mary phoned?' Alison was surprised. 'Did she leave a message?'

'No, though I did ask. When I told her Dad had gone to the station to fetch you, she said she'd phone back.'

Dear, concerned Mary! Probably wanting to make sure that Alison had got home safely.

They had almost finished their meal when the telephone rang.

'It's Mary again,' said Lynn, who had gone to answer the call.

'Mary!' said Alison gladly into the telephone.

'Alison? Oh, Alison, I'm so glad I reached you!' There was urgency in Mary's voice.

In a second, Alison was tense. *'What's wrong?'*

'There's been a bit of an accident.'

Clint! Alison knew it even before Mary said his name. In a second the blood had drained from her cheeks.

'Alison, it's Clint. He's hurt.'

'Oh God! Is he . . .' Alison could not bring herself to say the word.

'He's all right—I should have said that right away. I'm sorry, Alison, I didn't mean to scare you like that.'

'How bad is it?' White-knuckled, Alison gripped the phone.

'The doctors seem to think he has concussion, and a couple of ribs maybe fractured. He...he's unconscious.'

'Unconscious? That's terrible! Mary, what happened?'

'Well, actually...' Mary's voice had changed somewhat, 'it seems he was running.'

'Running? I don't understand... Where is he?'

'In hospital, in the town. I thought you'd want to know.'

'Yes, of course!' Alison put her free hand to a suddenly throbbing head. 'When did it happen?'

'Yesterday. I'd have phoned you earlier, but I didn't think you'd have got home until now. Alison, will you come and see him?'

'I'll be there the moment I can,' she promised unsteadily.

Lifeless fingers dropped the receiver back in its cradle. Alison's face was very pale as she turned to Lynn, who had come up behind her. 'It's Clint—Clint Demaine. He's been in an accident. I have to go to him!'

'Alison...?' There was a question in her sister's face.

'Yes, I love him. I love him so much that I don't know what I'll do if he...' She stopped. 'But Mary said he's all right. He has to be all right!'

Alison's father took one look at his daughter's face when she returned to the kitchen and told her parents what had happened, then said that he would drive her to the mountains himself. They set out almost immediately.

It was a long journey, the same one she had taken all those weeks ago with Clint. It was late afternoon when they left the village, so it grew dark quite soon, but they went on driving. And all the way Alison thought about the man she loved, and prayed that he would be all right.

It was early dawn when they reached the hospital. Mary and Virginia were waiting for her, looking tired, as if they'd spent the night keeping vigil.

Quickly Alison introduced her father. Then she said, 'Tell me about Clint!'

Mary glanced at Virginia. 'Would you mind very much if I talked to Alison alone?'

'No, of course not.' Virginia looked unusually subdued as she turned to Alison's father. 'You must have had a tiring journey out here, Mr Lenox. Can I go and get you some coffee?'

Alison had no time to wonder about this new civil Virginia, no mind to, either. All that mattered was Clint.

'Where is he?' she asked tersely, when she and Mary were alone.

'Down the passage, in a private room.' Mary touched Alison's arm. 'I'll take you to him in a minute, but first I think you should know what happened.'

'Couldn't we talk later? Right now I just want to see Clint.'

'There's something I think you should know before you see him. Besides'—Mary gave a tired smile—'you don't look too good yourself. You got here so quickly, did you stop to eat or rest?'

'Not for long,' Alison admitted.

'Well then, I think you should have something.' And, as Alison made a move to protest, 'You'll be no use to anyone if you flake out next. There's a little visitors' room along the passage. You can eat while I talk.'

Only when Alison was seated in a deep armchair, with a cup of coffee and a plate of sandwiches on a small table by her side, did Mary talk.

'Clint went after you,' she told her.

Alison almost dropped the cup she was holding. 'He did *what*?'

'You'd been gone a while when he noticed that you were missing. We were all so busy until then, getting ready to close up the camp, that nobody knew you were gone. It was already quite late when Clint said it was time to call it a day and go to the hotel.'

'The farewell party...'

'I kept wondering when to tell him about you. I thought I'd wait till the time seemed right—but in the end things took a different course. Clint went to your cabin.'

'Why?'

'I don't know. Anyway, he realised that you'd packed and gone. He came out looking frantic.'

Alison stared at her. 'Frantic?'

'You should have seen him! His eyes were wild, and his face was so white that I thought he'd faint. He was one distraught man.'

'I really didn't think I was hurting him,' Alison said painfully.

'He sent for me. He demanded to know what the hell was going on. I suppose he realised that if anyone knew where you'd gone it would be me.'

'What did you tell him?'

'That you were getting a lift into town with the van.'

'What...what did he say to that?' Alison's voice was unsteady.

'When he'd finished swearing, and my goodness, does that man know some choice words!'—there was mischief in Mary's smile for the first time—'he said he was going after you.'

'Did he think he'd be able to stop me?'

Mary nodded. 'Yes, I think so.'

'I see...'

'He shot the Porsche out of the camp grounds at one heck of a speed. I suppose he was determined to get to you before the train left.'

'He went into another car?' Alison asked through stiff lips.

'No, it wasn't a motor accident, I thought I told you that on the phone.' Mary reached out a sympathetic hand. 'He got to the station, Alison. We're not sure whether Clint thought you were on a train that was just leaving, but for some reason he started to run. And then, according to a witness, he hit a slick of oil and slipped.'

'Oh, no!' Alison explained.

'He was running so fast that he fell quite hard, and he must have hit his head on the ground. Fortunately, someone recognised him, and contacted the camp.'

'Is he still unconscious?' Alison whispered.

'Yes, it's odd. He hasn't opened his eyes or said a word since the accident.' Mary hesitated. 'The doctors don't know why.'

Alison had had a few sips of coffee and eaten one of the cheese sandwiches Mary had brought her. It was as much as she was going to have.

She stood up abruptly. 'I want to see him now.'

Clint was lying all alone in a small private room. A nurse stood by his bed, writing something on a chart. When Alison opened the door and peeped inside, the nurse glanced at her enquiringly.

'You must be Miss Lenox? Your friend said you'd be coming.'

Alison looked across at the figure lying motionless in the bed. 'How is he?' she asked unsteadily.

'Not too bad, considering the knock he took. It could have been a lot worse.'

'Mary said he hasn't spoken...'

'No, he hasn't. For some reason he just lies there. We don't know why. We're all hoping he'll respond to you.'

The nurse threw her a compassionate look. 'That's why we're letting you see him now, even though it's not visiting hour.'

'May I stay with him as long as I like?' asked Alison, knowing that she would stay by Clint's bed, no matter what the nurse said.

'Yes, of course. Look, there's the bell—don't hesitate to ring if you need help.'

When the door had closed behind the white-clad figure, Alison stood beside Clint and looked down at him.

He was lying so still. His face was pale despite his tan, and beneath his eyes the skin was smudged.

Quietly she drew up a chair beside the bed and sat down. Then she laid a hand gently over one of his.

This was not the dynamic, confident man Alison had fought so hard against loving. Clint looked so vulnerable that her heart went out to him, and a knot of pain filled her chest.

Suddenly it didn't seem to matter a bit that she had seen him kissing Virginia. All she knew was that there were things she had to say to him.

Softly she began to talk. 'Clint, this is me—Alison. You're hurt, my darling. You've been in an accident, and I came here to be with you.'

There was no response from him. He lay as still as before, long eyelashes resting on the smudged skin, his hand limp and unmoving beneath hers.

Alison trembled. Her eyes were wet, and her voice was choked with tears as she went on.

'It's all my fault. If I hadn't gone off without telling you, you wouldn't have tried to stop me, and you wouldn't be lying here now.'

She began to stroke his hand. 'I love you so much, Clint. You're my whole life. I didn't want to fall in love with you. I tried so hard to fight it, but I know now that I must have been in love with you almost from the beginning. I was going to tell you how I felt after the party at the hotel. But then...'

She stopped as tears threatened to close her throat, but she tried hard to swallow down on them. It was important that she go on talking to him. She hoped desperately that he would hear her, and would respond to her voice.

Standing up, she bent and kissed his mouth, willing him to show some sign of life, but the lips which had so often seduced her with their sweetness remained still against hers.

Picking up Clint's hand, she began to kiss it, first the palm, then each of the fingers. If he could not hear her, perhaps she could bring him back to consciousness with her touch.

Presently, a little desperate now, she put down his hand and went to the window. Somehow she had to get through to him. She would just have to talk to him until he heard her. There was no other way.

Abruptly she swung from the window and looked towards the bed—only to gasp in shocked amazement. For Clint's eyes were open, and he was watching her.

'Clint!' She was beside him in a moment. 'Oh, Clint, you're awake!'

'Yes, my Alison.'

'I've been sitting here talking to you, wishing you'd hear me.'

Incredibly, there was the hint of a smile in his eyes. 'I heard you.'

'You *did*?' She looked at him in amazement. 'How much did you hear?'

'Enough, darling.'

'But you didn't let on.'

'I know. I was hoping you'd say a little more.'

She stared at him. 'Do you mean to say you deliberately lay here listening, never letting on that you could hear me?'

'Yes.' He didn't even have the grace to look ashamed.

'Good heavens, Clint, you're a fraud!'

'Would you have said those very interesting things if you'd known I could hear you?'

Her colour was suddenly high. 'Yes—though I might have toned them down a bit.'

'Well,' he drawled, 'this *is* a change. Now I really am glad I decided to remain unconscious. That way I heard the lot without any toning.'

'*Decided* to remain unconscious, Clint?' she queried.

'I'm afraid so.'

'Then you know where you are, and what's happened to you?'

'I know I'm in a hospital, and that I had an accident of some kind. I even remember...' He frowned. 'Some of it's a little hazy, but the fact is, I've been awake for some time.'

Alison was bewildered. 'I don't understand. Why didn't you respond when people tried to speak to you? Mary and Virginia, the doctors and nurses. You must have known they'd be concerned about you.'

'I would have spoken, but I kept hoping that sooner or later someone would have the sense to call for you.' His eyes gleamed. 'I presume someone did.'

'Mary phoned.' Alison looked down at the man she loved. 'How much do you remember, Clint?'

'A little. I went to your cabin, but you'd gone, without as much as a word to me. Mary said you were catching a train, and I realised I had to stop you.' He paused a moment, making an obvious effort to think back. 'I remember... jumping into my car. I knew I had to get to the train before you did. And then... I got to the station, and I think... yes, there was a train that was just leaving. I didn't know if you were on it.' He looked very tired suddenly. 'The rest is a blank, I'm afraid.'

When Alison had told him the remainder of the story, he looked exasperated. 'I slipped? What a *stupid* thing to do!'

Yesterday Alison had allowed hurt pride to get the better of her, but not today.

'I was the stupid one,' she said quietly. 'I shouldn't have run away from Bushveld. I blame myself, Clint. First Timmy was hurt, now you.'

'Both freak accidents—you can't be blamed for either of them.' Incredibly, he laughed.

It was so good to hear the sound that she was able to say, 'Now what about this business of playing unconscious? Don't you have any scruples, Clint?'

'Not a single one where you're concerned, my darling Alison. And certainly not after all we've been through. Whatever happened to me yesterday was worth it, if it brought you to my bedside and caused you to say all those very nice things.'

She tensed. 'Clint...'

'Why did you leave, Alison?'

Alison's cheeks were hot. 'I saw you with Virginia, in your cabin. You were kissing...'

Something moved in Clint's eyes, and his breath was a hiss. 'Good heavens! So it was that—the kiss! It never occurred to me that you might have seen it.'

'It hurt,' Alison said painfully.

'It shouldn't have. You'll realise that when I tell you about it. But first,' Clint said very softly, 'I want to know what happened to the girl who was never going to be jealous again.'

'She fell in love.' Alison's voice was very low. 'If you heard as much as you say you did, then you know that.'

He grinned. But there was something other than amusement in his eyes, a naked expression. Suddenly the blood was singing in her veins.

'Yes, I do know,' he said.

'Do you mind?' she asked urgently.

'*Mind?*' His voice was ragged. 'Come and put your head on the pillow beside me, Alison. I don't think I can hold you just yet, but we can still be close.'

'The nurse won't like it,' Alison said mischievously.

'It doesn't matter. All that matters is you and me.'

She bent towards him, careful not to lie where she could hurt him, but laying her head as close as she could beside his on the pillow. Weak Clint might be, and unable to hold her, yet still his nearness set her senses whirling. For a while they lay quite still, with Alison's lips nuzzling his throat.

When Clint spoke at last, his breath fanned her lips. 'I love you, my darling Alison.'

'*You do?*' She raised her head and looked down at him.

'I do, darling. I fell in love with you on our trip down to Bushveld all those weeks ago. I never knew I could love a woman as much as I love you.'

'Clint!' Joy was a wild thing, burgeoning inside her, filling her, consuming her. She couldn't believe what she was hearing. 'You never said anything.'

'I didn't dare to. The Alison I knew at the start would have been frightened out of her wits if I'd told her how I felt about her.'

'That's true,' she admitted ruefully.

He tried to turn to her on the pillow, winced and lay still. 'You'll have to do all the kissing for now, darling.'

Her kisses were gentle. She kissed his lips, his eyes, then his lips again.

At last she said, 'I don't want to tire you. Perhaps I should leave you for a while.'

'Don't you dare! There are things I've waited too long to say to you. I love you so much, my darling Alison. You're part of me, part of my blood, part of my life. I can't imagine a life that doesn't have you in it.'

'I only wish I'd known all along,' she sighed.

'No, darling, it's better that you didn't. You were so frightened of loving—so distrustful of it—that we wouldn't have had a chance together.'

She thought about that for a moment. 'You're probably right,' she agreed.

'I kept hoping you'd come to understand that you loved me, but I knew I couldn't rush you. Do you remember asking me why I didn't write or phone when I was away on the business trip? That was the reason. I wanted you to have some time alone, so that you could think about your feelings.'

'I didn't realise...'

'I was determined that when you finally came to me, you'd know it wasn't on the rebound from Raymond.'

'It was never rebound, Clint.' Alison was quiet a moment. Then she said, 'You were right, you know—I was never in love with Raymond. It really was a brother-sister relationship all along, and I didn't know it. I ran into them at the station when I arrived home, Raymond and Edna together, and I didn't feel a thing—except for affection for a very dear friend.'

'I'm relieved to hear it,' Clint said quietly.

'I think Raymond was, too.' She felt as if there was was nothing she could not say to him. Now and for ever.

'It's you I love, Clint,' she said. 'Only you.'

He managed to move his head a little closer to hers. 'And I'll never love anyone but you, my darling Alison.'

She wanted nothing more than to give herself up completely to the utter happiness of the moment, but there was something she had to say first.

'I have to tell you, Clint, I was so jealous of Virginia.'

'The girl who was never going to be jealous again! I asked you once if you were jealous, and you denied it.'

'Because to admit it would have been admitting to myself that I loved you.' She was quiet a moment as she remembered. 'That night at the hotel, when I saw you together, I realised for the first time that I was jealous. I wanted to die. Even then I tried so hard to fight being in love with you'—she grinned—'and got myself thrown in the swimming-pool fully-dressed for my efforts!'

'Brian's party.' Laughter bubbled in Clint's throat. ''I always wondered what got into you that night.'

'Now you know. All along I was fighting myself far more than I was fighting you—you were right about that. But I thought I could cope. And then yesterday, when I saw you and Virginia kissing, I knew I couldn't bear to share you.'

'You'll never have to share me, that's a promise,' Clint told her. 'I said I would tell you why I was kissing Virginia?'

The new Alison said, 'Yes, I want to know.'

'She'd just heard the news that she'd done well on her psychology thesis, that she was going to get a wonderful job as a result of it. She's worked so hard, Alison, and I was happy for her.'

'Oh...' Alison whispered inadequately.

'There was no sex in the kiss, darling. It was a congratulatory kiss, it never went further that.'

She believed him. 'But there used to be something...'

'We used to date. I like Virginia, and she's still a good friend, but it's never been serious.'

It had been more serious for Virginia, Alison knew. And she hoped the boost to Virginia's career would be some consolation for the loss of Clint in her life.

'So that's the real reason you kept defending her,' she said wryly. 'I always sensed there was more to it than just the fact that she was a competent camp director.'

'Maybe it was a double reason,' Clint conceded. 'I told Virginia how I felt about you.' He grinned. 'After the kiss! You might even have heard me if you'd waited.'

'I've behaved like an idiot,' Alison reproached herself.

'You behaved like a girl who'd been hurt.'

'Yes...' she agreed.

'That's all over now. Alison, when Linda died I thought I would never love again, and for nine years I didn't. There were women here and there, but they were always just friends—like Virginia. And then I met you, and all of a sudden I was so deeply in love that I couldn't think straight. It's been so hard not to make love to you, my darling—especially when I was beginning to hope you were ready for it.'

'I *was* ready. That was the other thing I was going to tell you after the party—that I wanted you to make love to me.'

'Do you mean that? Good lord! I can feel my blood pressure shooting up.'

'Careful!' teased Alison. 'The nurse might have something to say about that.'

He laughed. 'I think she'd be happy to know I'd recovered consciousness and was getting back to normal so quickly.'

And then his voice altered. 'I told you I went to your cabin and found you gone. I'd come to tell you I was in love with you.'

'Oh, Clint!' Alison thought she had never been quite as happy as she was at this moment. 'If only I'd been there!'

'All along I promised myself to give you all the time you needed to get over Raymond. But camp had ended, and I knew I couldn't wait any longer. Alison darling, I was going to ask you to marry me.'

Joy made the blood pound in her veins. She lifted herself on the pillow and kissed him lingeringly.

'You're a witch,' he groaned. 'A maddening, utterly desirable little witch. I'm dying to make love to you, my darling. Do you know what it's like to know that I can't?'

'You'll just have to get better quickly.'

'Will you marry me if I do?'

Her pulse was beating a crazy tattoo. 'Yes! Yes, my darling, I want so much to be your wife.'

'You can still have your stables,' Clint promised.

'Oh, Clint, I'd like that!'

'You already own the lovely horse you wanted so badly.'

'I do?' She looked at him disbelievingly.

'I bought it for you. It's being boarded till you're ready for it.'

'I don't know what to say.' Her voice was ragged.

'You don't need to say anything. Just kiss me again.'

She did—more provocatively this time, letting her tongue trace the outline of his lips, laughing softly when he groaned.

'Start making plans,' he ordered, 'because I intend to get out of this place quickly.'

'I hope the counsellors can all make it to the wedding,' said Alison happily. 'And I'd like Mary and my sister Lynn to be my bridesmaids. Clint, do you think Timmy would be able to come?' she added.

'We'll have to convince his parents to bring him. We couldn't have a wedding without your Timmy.'

'My father is in the waiting-room with Mary and Virginia. I know he'll want to meet you.'

'I want to meet my future father-in-law, too. I'll ask him for your hand, and if he says no, I'll tell him you've given it to me already.'

'I'll call him.'

'Kiss me again first,' demanded Clint.

She did so. And this time he was even able to reciprocate—so thoroughly that when the nurse opened the door to see how her patient was doing, neither Clint nor Alison were aware of her presence.

It was amazing what miracles love could bring about, reflected the nurse, as she closed the door quietly, and left them to it.

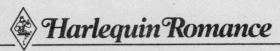 *Harlequin Romance*

Coming Next Month

2971 REMEMBER, IN JAMAICA Katherine Arthur
For three years Claire has battled with her boss over his violent temper, impossible dreams and insane schedules. Suddenly, once she agrees to the working trip in Jamaica, Terrill changes into a pussycat. Claire can't help feeling suspicious.

2972 NO LOVE IN RETURN Elizabeth Barnes
The only reason Eve has worked as a model is to pay for her brother's education. To the imperious Jackson Sinclair, however, *model* is synonymous with *gold digger*. And there seems to be no way to persuade him he's wrong.

2973 SNOWFIRE Dana James
Beth can't pass up the chance to be official photographer on an Iceland expedition, though she's stunned to find her estranged husband, Dr. Allan Bryce, as leader. Even more shocking is the realization that Allan thinks he was the injured party!

2974 SYMPATHETIC STRANGERS Annabel Murray
Recently widowed Sandra begins to build a new life for herself and her young twins by helping friends of her mother's in Kent. Yet when lord of the manor Griff Faversham pursues her, she refuses to consider marriage to another wealthy man.

2975 BED, BREAKFAST & BEDLAM Marcella Thompson
In helping Bea McNair establish an Ozark Mountain retreat for Bea's ailing friends, Janet dismisses Lucas McNair's plan to move his mother to a Little Rock retirement home. There's no dismissing Lucas, though, when he descends upon her like a wrathful God.

2976 MOWANA MAGIC Margaret Way
Ally can't deny the attraction between herself and the powerful Kiall Lancaster, despite his mistrust of her. Common sense tells her to leave. But first she determines to straighten out Kiall's chauvinistic attitude. Not an easy task!

Available in April wherever paperback books are sold, or through Harlequin Reader Service:

In the U.S.
901 Fuhrmann Blvd.
P.O. Box 1397
Buffalo, N.Y. 14240-1397

In Canada
P.O. Box 603
Fort Erie, Ontario
L2A 5X3

Harlequin Regency Romance™

Romance the way it was *always* meant to be!

The time is 1811, when a Regent Prince rules the empire. The place is London, the glittering capital where rakish dukes and dazzling debutantes scheme and flirt in a dangerously exciting game. Where marriage is the passport to wealth and power, yet every girl hopes secretly for love....

Welcome to Harlequin Regency Romance where reading is an adventure and romance is *not* just a thing of the past! Two delightful books a month, beginning May '89.

Available wherever Harlequin Books are sold.

Have You Ever Wondered If You Could Write A Harlequin Novel?

Here's great news—Harlequin is offering a series of cassette tapes to help you do just that. Written by Harlequin editors, these tapes give practical advice on how to make your characters—and your story— come alive. There's a tape for each contemporary romance series Harlequin publishes.

Mail order only

All sales final